THE KINGDOM

Also by Fuminori Nakamura

The Gun

The Thief

Evil and the Mask

Last Winter, We Parted

THE
KINGDOM

FUMINORI
NAKAMURA

Translated from the Japanese by Kalau Almony

Copyright © 2011 by Fuminori Nakamura
English translation © 2016 by Kalau Almony

First published in Japanese in 2011 by Kawadeshobo-Shinsha.
First published in English in 2016 by Soho Press.

Soho Press
853 Broadway
New York, NY 10003

Library of Congress Cataloging-in-Publication Data
Nakamura, Fuminori, 1977–
Almony, Kalau, translator.
The kingdom / Fuminori Nakamura;
translated from the Japanese by Kalau Almony.

ISBN 978-1-61695-592-2
eISBN 978-1-61695-593-9

1. Organized crime—Japan—Fiction. I. Title
PL873.5.A339 O3613 2016 (print) PL873.5.A339 (ebook)
DDC 895.6/36—dc23   2015048583

Interior design by Janine Agro, Soho Press, Inc.

Printed in the United States of America

10 9 8 7 6 5 4 3 2 1

THE KINGDOM

1.

WHEN DID I realize I would never get what I wanted most?

Maybe I was in my twenties. Or maybe I was a child, just old enough to make sense of the world. Back when I did nothing but glare at everyone around me, what I wanted most was far away. It was not something tangible. It made my skin burn. It ignored all the rules. It went beyond morals and reason. It was something that could overturn the foundations of everything I thought my life would become. I wonder if I still want it. What would I do if I got it?

THE MAN IN front of me, bathed in blue light, was looking at me. I smiled and watched the passion build in his eyes. He glanced at my chest, then returned his gaze to my face. He acted relaxed as he closed in on me one step at a time.

"I can't believe it. I'd never have thought you were a prostitute."

Properly speaking, I'm not a prostitute, but I smiled anyway. The man slid his fingers between mine.

"I don't tell anyone I don't like," I said. "It's wonderful. Much better than watching TV."

I pressed my body against his and kissed his neck. I held his hand gently, and brought it up to my chest. He touched my chest reluctantly. Though I didn't feel anything special, I began to mix heavy breathing into my speech.

". . . You can forget it all. Do what you want to me. Mmm . . . Whatever you want."

His temperature rose. Humans do not always make

rational decisions. When our senses are shaken, we become defenseless. I felt the hand on my breast growing bolder. I stroked the man's lips with my finger, and put a pill in his mouth.

"What's this?"

"It's kind of like a mild Viagra. You can get it at any pharmacy, but it's pretty good."

I stretched my legs from my short skirt and forced them between his. I kissed his neck, wrapped my arms around him, and whispered, "Let's do it. Let's do it." With my lips pressed against his neck, I felt him swallow the pill. He pushed me violently onto the bed. He was completely engrossed in me. I held his body against my chest. The feeling that I was in control of him got me hot. There was no sign of his turning back. I pretended to fool around, avoided his kisses, and wrapped my arms around his neck. I gently petted the man's head. His face was buried in my chest. I continued stroking his head until he stopped moving.

I watched the man with detachment as his hands began to slow. Strangely, looking into those half-closed eyes, I got hot again at my own act of treachery. The heat traveled through my body, raising my pulse and causing sounds of joy to gurgle up from deep inside me. I slowly brought my mouth to his ear.

"Don't worry. It's not poison."

There was something evil in the glow of the room's blue lights. I felt the weight of the man on top of me. He could no longer move. His eyes were closed. I stared long into his face. I realized that I wanted him. I wanted the passion he had until a moment ago. I wanted his shoulders, which were quite muscular for his age, and his naturally tan face. I got out from under his body, sat in a chair, and lit a cigarette. I had to wait like this until he fell into a deep sleep.

It was raining outside.

The quiet rising up from the man's body joined the sound of the rain.

I carefully removed the man's light blue shirt, and then slowly pulled his white tank top off over his head. His tanned chest was broad, like I thought it would be. I took off my blouse, so I only had on a bra, and put on sunglasses. I lay in bed next to the topless man, put his arm under my head, and took several pictures of us head on. I also recorded a video. Last time, when my victim was a politician, I understood why I'd been hired. Why anyone needed these kinds of pictures of a TV anchor, I didn't know. I expected he thought I was just a normal person drinking in that bar. He probably hadn't thought I'd been watching him the whole time.

After carefully redressing him, my job was done. I'd created a point of weakness in his life. I took some money from his wallet and put it in my own. I saw a receipt from an expensive Japanese restaurant, and his gym membership card. I lit another cigarette, and wrote a message on the hotel's notepad.

"I didn't touch your cards. Procuring prostitutes is illegal . . . I'm sure you understand."

The very existence of prostitutes is illegal, so when he'd tried to buy me, he'd become a criminal, too. He had been seduced into criminality. Who with any standing in society would go to the police over this much money? When he read the note I left, he'd think only his money was stolen. But really, he'd be wrong.

The blue lights in the hotel room were still letting off their evil glow. What were those lights illuminating?

Maybe the petty crime of this man who had tried to buy me, even though he had a ring on his finger? Or maybe, my existence.

I carefully fixed my makeup in the bathroom, put on my coat, and left the room. Though the building didn't stand out much, on the inside it was a luxury love hotel. I exited the elevator, and as I walked past the front desk, Saito said, "Good night." At places like this, you can only see the wrists of whoever's working the front desk, but I happen to know Saito has a very handsome face.

"You too. Sorry if he makes a fuss."

"It'll be fine."

The lobby's huge, gaudy chandelier made me feel better. Its showiness seemed to mock the world. When I left the hotel, the men walking the late-night streets looked at me, their gazes crossing one another's, full of all kinds of emotions. I walked slowly through all of those gazes. A black car was parked on the side of the hotel like it was meant to be there. It reflected, or maybe repelled, the neon lights. It was a luxury car. Some brand I didn't know. I opened the door and got in. The heater wasn't even on inside.

The man in the driver's seat didn't say anything when I got in. He says his name is Yata, but that's probably not his real name. When I showed him the digital camera, he took it casually and put it in his attaché case. Yata's eyes are small, and his face is plain, but he has beautiful fingers.

"You can get the pictures of him going in from Saito."

"I already got them."

The inside of the car was freezing. We were cut off from the noise of the night.

"But . . . Why a TV anchor?"

"One of your best qualities is that you don't pry. Remember that."

He gave me an envelope full of money, but I didn't need it much anymore.

I got out of the car and turned my back to it as Yata stepped on the gas. I walked through the city. The heat from pulling that man close to me, and the heat from betraying him, still lingered in my body. A tout I knew by face started talking to me. In front of a hotel, a Chinese woman was negotiating with a client. There were older men walking with younger girls, and older women walking with younger men. The obscene neon. The light that makes fun of the world. Night makes people's desires take on physical form. Night forgives people for letting loose the desires they keep buried inside.

The moon shone down from over my head, casting its light on the neon's glow. After the sun sets, the moon steals its light to illuminate our existence.

2.

I WOKE TO an afterimage floating before my eyes.

It changed from red to green. The transparent image looked like haphazardly flung paint, and it continued to tremble even when I closed my eyes. I had forgotten what I dreamed last night, but I thought that dream must have been some kind of stain seeping out from deep within me. Then I realized I had left my bedside lamp on, and it had caused the afterimage. My room was overly big. My chest was sweating.

I turned on the TV, and the anchor I photographed last night was on. He smiled and spoke well. There was nothing particularly strange about him. The show didn't rouse my attention, so I turned off the TV. When did I stop being able to follow all the text streaming busily across the screen?

I took a shower, went to the kitchen, and ate half of a roll I had bought. The clock said 6 P.M. Lots of people have told me I should get a pet. The size of my room probably makes me look even more alone. But I never wanted to have to go through something close to me losing its life again. Since Eri and that boy died, I have become extremely sensitive to life. Life is terrifying.

I felt like I washed myself cleaner than usual. I was going to meet Hasegawa. A few days before, he'd suddenly called out and stopped me on the stairs in front of the train station's ticket gates. "Is that you, Yurika?" he asked, and as I was preparing to lie to him, he said he was Hasegawa. I placed him right away because he was wearing a blue down jacket. Under that down jacket, he had on a sweater of the same color. That was the color of the hand-me-down sweater he always used to wear when we were at the orphanage, back when we were in elementary school. Even though that sweater was old, on him it looked pristine. I don't know whose it used to be, but it probably suited Hasegawa better.

"When we're grown up," Hasegawa once told me, "we'll show everyone. Until then, no backing down."

Regardless, I guess people really do bump into each other like that. I left my room. For a second, I wasn't sure whether I should, but I put my lucky knife in my bag. I picked clothes that weren't too revealing, and put on the rings and piercings that I liked. The moon was out.

HASEGAWA HAD ASKED me to come to a bar in Ikebukuro. It was overflowing with customers. "It's dirty, but the food is good," Hasegawa had told me in a text message. The place was definitely plain, and the tables and counter looked painfully scratched-up and dented.

Crowds of drunk people moved through the smoke-filled shop. I'm not sure why, but I thought it would be nice if this was what the world was like after death. The dead all get drunk somewhere, surrounded by a white haze. They sing songs and never notice that they are gradually disappearing. But then where would the children go? Children can't get drunk, so they'd have to remain conscious of themselves as they disappear.

Hasegawa raised his hand. He was sitting at a table in the back. His blue down jacket was immaculate. Hasegawa might have been the person I'd spoken to most at the orphanage. I was quiet, though, so we still probably hadn't talked that much. When I think back, he had been a fast runner. These memories felt sentimental, but I couldn't feel anything else, probably because I was dried up. I smiled and approached the table.

"Yurika. It feels strange to say your name."

"It shouldn't."

"It's just, well, it's been a long time."

I drank beer and stared at the yakitori and whatever boiled dish Hasegawa ordered. I watched him eating innocently, like everything was delicious, and thought he must get a lot of girls. His nails were cut short, and his fingers were thin and lovely. His face showed the determination of someone who made it through some kind of trouble, but then he would suddenly smile like a defenseless child. He seemed like he hadn't changed since we were kids. I wondered if he was still fast.

"Um." It had been bothering me, so I decided to ask him. "How did you recognize me in that crowd?"

"I think it was the way you walk."

Hasegawa swallowed something and looked at me sweetly.

"Actually, I saw you in the same spot last week. But I didn't have the courage to say anything. You walk fast, Yurika. You move your body like everyone around you is an obstacle and you have to dodge them all. But you're not looking down on everyone, it's more . . . How should I put it? . . . It's like you're so focused on where you're going, and you want to get there fast. The way you walk, it's like . . . the opposite of cowardice."

He said that and smiled.

"I've always been a coward, you know. I'm a coward, but I hate to lose."

I may not be a coward anymore. But that's because being a coward is the same as having the will to live.

"Now I'm working as an interpreter for tourists. And

on the weekends I work at the orphanage. I'm just a volunteer, though. I heard about Shota."

I felt a slight trembling deep within my chest. I was buzzing on the inside.

"You did all that even though he wasn't your child. That was so amazing of you . . . Or, well, that's not what I mean. Everyone was surprised at all that money . . . Oh, I'm sorry . . ."

I guessed what I must have looked like based on his panicked expression. I must not have gotten over it yet. I smiled at him to let him know that he didn't have to worry.

The outlines of all the drunk customers blurred in the white smoke. If there is only nothingness after death, what's the point of this world?

"No, don't worry about it. So, you're helping out at the orphanage? That's great."

"Well, Yurika, I was wondering if you'd want to, too. I heard about what you did, and . . . If you came, we could see each other every weekend."

I looked straight at him. His kindhearted eyes got me hot all of a sudden. If I entwined my legs with his under the table, what kind of face would he make? He mistook me for good-natured. I wanted to ruin him. He had been by my side since I was a child thrown out into the world without knowing anything. I wanted to dirty all of his beautiful memories. He would probably be depressed to know the woman I actually am, but in the end, he'd probably try to sleep with me. It would probably be all right to sleep with him. But which would be more intense? The heat when he slept with me, or the heat from making him obsessed with me, then betraying him, and ruining this good man's life?

I sensed hatred in my thoughts, so I took my eyes off of him. At the very least, I don't want to think about people from the orphanage that way.

". . . And he refused, but he said he could come somewhere nearby . . . Do you mind if I invite him?"

I realized Hasegawa had been talking. All of a sudden, I could hear the buzz of the shop.

"Who?"

"Huh? Oh, the new director of the orphanage. When we were there, the director was Mr. Nishida, and during Shota's time it was Mr. Kataoka, right?

The new director's name is Mr. Kondo. When I said I was going to come meet you tonight, he said he wanted to meet you too. When he heard about what you did for Shota, he said he'd love to meet anyone from the orphanage who did something like that. He's a good man. You should really come help out, too."

After that, I became anxious. I was fuzzy-headed. Kondo joined us at the restaurant, and I worried I hadn't properly greeted him. He wore a brown jacket and black hat. He was tall and had wide shoulders. He took a seat in one of the bar's small chairs. I wondered why people who knew about that kid were suddenly showing up in front of me now. I tried to hide my wild emotions and had no choice but to smile at Kondo and Hasegawa.

Kondo said something nice about me and ordered a beer, saying he'd just have one drink. He stared at me. His appearance was somewhat intimidating, but if he was the director of an orphanage, he must have been good deep down. What kind of face would he make if he knew what I do now? The area around us blurred white again from all the customers' smoke. Kondo told me about the current state of the orphanage and the kids there. I wanted to cover my ears. I grew more upset, and I couldn't look at him properly. I'm not sure why, but I was bad at dealing with this kind of man. I continued to smile evasively.

"Well, it's bad of me to interfere with Hasegawa's love life, so I'll leave you two."

Hasegawa got a bit flustered, and Kondo handed him several bills, smiling. I kept smiling emotionlessly. The familiar warmth of good people. But I was far removed from that warmth.

"Oh, no . . . He always does this. He shows up for a second, and then just leaves . . . And he says all sorts of nonsense."

"Ha ha. But he's an interesting guy."

"Yeah. He may look like a bruiser, but he's actually a good person. Really, if you're free, come this weekend. I'm sure Mr. Kondo would be happy."

He closed his mouth and scratched his ear. Suddenly, my heart began to race. I had been holding off on smoking, but now I instinctively began searching for my cigarettes to calm myself down. Maybe I'd been wrong. I looked at Hasegawa again, but I couldn't tell anymore.

I had thought he stopped talking because he was embarrassed, but his eyes were very cold. He looked, for just a second, like someone I had never seen before. Why do I get shaken up so quickly over such small things? He began to make me nervous just sitting in front of me, but I forced a smile, taking short breaths so he wouldn't notice.

"Hey, do you remember that time we kissed in the storage closet?" I asked.

He stared at me kindly, and said, "When I think about it now, it's kind of embarrassing."

What was he saying? We never did that. My heart beat even faster.

HE SAID HE would see me to the station, and I couldn't refuse. I began to lose confidence in my own memories. Hasegawa and I were often together at the orphanage, but when I tried to remember his face, the details were hazy. I couldn't remember clearly what he looked like. This must have been Hasegawa, but if he hadn't told me his name, would I have recognized him? I tried to remember the other kids from the orphanage. I could remember their faces, but I had a hard time imagining what they'd look like grown up. And why had he played along with my lie? Did he do it to hide the fact that he'd forgotten? If he wasn't Hasegawa, why would he invite me out like this? I didn't get it. My head began to hurt. I was questioning too much. I've always been like this. Thinking this much is practically the same as being crazy. I let out a small sigh. Something wasn't exactly right, but this man definitely had Hasegawa's face.

I waved back at Hasegawa, and joined the crowd in the station. I wondered if he thought it was strange that I was going home even though it was only ten. I wanted to avoid crowded trains as much as possible. I continued to think about Hasegawa as I moved through the crowd. When I turned toward the taxi stand, someone tapped my shoulder. Startled, I turned around and a man was holding my lucky knife. I couldn't breathe, and pain shot through my chest.

"Why are you carrying this kind of thing around?"

He was wearing a black coat. He had a handsome face, but it was a bit too skinny. Why was he holding the knife I had in my bag?

"Excuse me?"

"Well, never mind."

The man returned the knife to me. At some point, my bag must have been opened.

"Why did you meet with that man in the brown jacket?"

"Huh?"

"Why did you meet with Kizaki?"

What was he talking about?

"Kizaki? The man I met was named Kondo. What is this about?"

"His name's not Kondo."

I realized the man was wearing expensive clothes. He didn't look suspicious. His fingers were kind of long, and his eyes were dark. For some reason, he seemed a bit irritated at himself for talking to me.

"Let me tell you one thing. You shouldn't get involved with that man."

"What?"

"How should I put it? He's a monster," he said. "Well, then." He tried to step away into the crowd. I stopped him.

"My knife. I didn't drop it, did I? Did you take it out of my bag?"

All the people around us were moving in every direction. The man looked at me silently.

"That's a strange way to communicate," I said.

His expression changed for just a second. But he disappeared into the movement of the crowd. I didn't understand what he was doing. He must have confused me for someone else.

3.

I WAS LEANING on the wall in the hallway of the sixth floor of the Imperial Hotel.

The elevator door opened, and an upset woman got off. She had a young face. She looked like she was still in college. She was wearing black stockings under blue denim shorts. I thought this must have been her, so I called out, "Kobayashi." Before selling her body, a woman worries about all the different looks she's getting. Even ones that don't exist. Either she listens to music to isolate herself, or she stares at the screen of her cell phone. But this woman just walked, upset. She was surprised, and turned to face me.

I was right—it was Kobayashi. I told her just what I was told to say.

"We don't need you anymore. Miyawaki told me to take care of this customer."

"What?"

"Sorry. Here's your cab fare. Aren't you lucky!"

She belonged to a prostitution ring. I had to secretly trade places with her, pretend to be a woman from this ring, and do my usual work. I wasn't sure, but Miyawaki was probably the ring's manager or something.

I could see the tension in the girl's face fade. She probably still wasn't used to this. Why was she doing this kind of work? She was probably looking at me, thinking the same thing.

I took off my sunglasses and pressed the room's buzzer. A man wearing a nightgown opened the door. It was the man from the picture I'd been given. I didn't know anything about him, except that he was the director of an independent administrative corporation.

His lips were too thick, his nose was big, and he was terribly fat. This would be a challenge. It wouldn't be like with the TV anchor.

Seeing the coldness in his eyes, I knew he had sadistic tendencies.

"Hey," he said, watching me as I entered the room. He seemed unsatisfied. "Aren't you going to get on your knees and bow? Isn't that the rule where you work? When you come in, first you get on your knees, bow, and then say, 'I look forward to serving you.'"

I smiled a little to keep from showing my displeasure.

"I'm sorry. I'm still new, so I didn't know."

I noticed him react to what I said. Why do men prefer amateur prostitutes? I kept talking.

"So please, teach me. This is from my company."

I took out a bottle. The label was that of some luxury health drink you could find in a drug store, but the contents were something else.

"I always say I don't need those. I can't trust 'em."

"But . . ." I made an embarrassed face and moistened my eyes. "It works pretty well. I don't know much about this work, and I want to enjoy myself, too. I want you to dominate me. I mean, I want to be treated like . . . Oh, this is embarrassing."

He looked at me with lustful eyes. There's nothing but unhappiness in being wanted by an ugly man.

"Please drink this . . . You'll be stronger."

This wasn't that other love hotel, so if I got myself into trouble, I wouldn't be able to get help from Saito at the front desk. I gripped the stun gun in my bag. If he approached me, I'd have no other choice but to wrap my arms around him and turn it on. But he drank the health drink like an idiot. He put the drink on the table, his lips wet. He smiled and tried to get closer to me. But the drug in that bottle was quick-acting. He lost his balance. I pushed him lightly over onto the bed, and sat on the sofa some ways away. He struggled to get up, but he didn't have the strength. That arrogant man looked like a bug to me. I lit a cigarette. The lights in the room shone orange. They illuminated this bug, about to fall asleep, and they illuminated unhappy me.

As I smoked my cigarette, I thought about the word "monster." For some reason the man who took my knife called Kondo a monster. I'd heard the same word a long time ago from Eri. She was my only friend, and that kid Shota's mother. Both she and that kid died, leaving me all alone again.

ERI AND I had worked together at an exclusive club in Tokyo. Before that, in a distant time I didn't know much about, she did something at a big food company in Nagoya.

"It was awful working there. It was a super male-centric company. I didn't go to a great college, but I'm tenacious, so I did my best and made something of a name for myself. But I wasn't married, and already over thirty. So they started spreading stupid rumors."

Eri had told me about it late at night in her apartment. It was an unpretentious, one-room apartment in Meguro. In the ashtray were the thin menthol cigarettes she always used to smoke, and in the bed in the corner slept Shota. At the time, she was thirty-eight and I was just over twenty.

"And then, I met a guy. He was young. Still in his twenties. I had dated a lot when I was younger, but for a while I had been avoiding men. I'd had some bad experiences . . . But that man was different. He's Shota's father."

Eri fell for him right away, but at first she couldn't accept him as her lover. It may have been because she was considerably older. Maybe making him wait was her way of trying to make up for that handicap and put herself in a superior position in their relationship. It also might have been fear, or because of the little pride she had. After being wooed at length, she gave in. She let herself surrender to his passion, and they became lovers. After they'd had sex only two or three times, Eri had already become his woman. She forgot about her pride and gave herself entirely to him. She depended on him, and she felt no discomfort in needing him for even little things.

"And then, he said, 'Let's get married.' Just when I was trying to convince myself it was the right time. I was scared by how happy I'd feel, fulfilling our relationship . . . I've never been as happy as I was in that moment."

He worked in Tokyo at a mid-level advertising agency. It wasn't a big company, but he had been given an important post even though he was still young. He was tall, and his eyes were big, but sometimes he'd squint like a child. He didn't dress up much, but he always looked clean, and he liked cars. The long-distance relationship was hard on Eri, but he came to Nagoya frequently. And now he wanted to get married and live in Tokyo.

Eri felt her current career path where she worked was hopeless, and she was tired. She was happy to quit her job. She wondered what kind of faces her disgusting bosses and the other female employees would make when she told them she was getting married. Eri immediately agreed to the man's suggestion. The man pulled her close and said, "You should tell all those bastards who've spread strange rumors about you, and all the younger girls that work there. Tell them you're going to quit because you're getting married."

He smiled. Eri was in a state of bliss. She quit the job that she'd been working for more than ten years, packed up her things, got rid of her furniture, and took her bag to the man's apartment in Tokyo. He said he would pay for the wedding, so Eri covered the honeymoon. Overjoyed, she made reservations for an expensive tour overseas. But it turned out the man actually had no job, had already been married for some time, and even had a kid. The room Eri arrived at was a weekly rental he had booked especially for that day.

"I didn't know what was happening. There, in that room, with him in front of me, I was dumbfounded. Wouldn't you be? I'd given up my job and career, gotten rid of all of my furniture, and come to Tokyo with nothing but this body of mine . . . I was way past thirty, and I thought I was going to get married."

If it had been a case of the man's not having the courage to leave his wife, if, when Eri finally came to Tokyo, he could only look at her with eyes full of despair, she would probably have been mad at his worthlessness, and feel angry at herself for being tricked. Or if he had been mocking her, if when she appeared naively he had laughed at her, she would have gotten mad at his cruel thoughtlessness, and been mad at herself for getting so obsessed. But what he did was different.

"He had this serious look on his face. I had never seen him look so serious before. I had lost everything. There was nothing more ridiculous or pathetic than me. He looked at me and sympathized. He cried."

Eri didn't understand what was happening. She couldn't understand because the man crying was the one who brought her there.

"And then his whole body started shaking . . . While he was staring at me . . . When I realized he was getting off, I was so scared I couldn't move. I had been tricked. I was pathetic. I had been completely ruined. And when he looked at me, at how hopeless I was, he got off. He even said, 'This is the most beautiful you've ever been.' He covered me with his body. He was so excited he ripped at my clothes, and fucked me violently."

When Eri said that, she looked off into the distance as though she were telling me about something that happened long ago. The white smoke from Eri's cigarette melted into the air as if it had given up.

"Sex with him had never been that violent. It was like he couldn't feel real desire except for a woman tortured to that extreme. He twisted my arms and pushed them over my head, and choked me over and over again, so hard. When I writhed in pain, he'd look at me with these sympathetic eyes, but still, he'd hurt me more. The more he sympathized with me, the more I thought myself pathetic, and the more he got off . . . He'd always been indifferent to sex, and never wanted to do it that much. But that was probably to save the novelty for that day. This had been his aim all along. In other words . . . What can I say? He was a monster. There are very few real monsters, and most people live their lives without ever meeting one. He was one. I was so scared I couldn't move. It was so scary. More than anything, the scariest part was . . . I felt it."

Eri was not drunk when she told this to me. She looked at me, her eyes earnest.

"I had never had sex that I felt so much. Until then, I had only had normal sex. If I got hurt, I'd stop being into it, and I hated fetishists. If I wasn't in the mood, I wouldn't do anything sexual. But even though I was crying, I came again and again. It was pathetic. It was the worst. But still, amidst all that, it was like someone lit a fire inside me. I thought that if he continued to abuse me . . . I don't know. Like I'd arrive at something. This white and hazy place, somewhere nearby where the essence of all humanity was waiting to get me. At some point, this keychain on my bag fell on the floor. I bought it on a trip with him. It was some small town's mascot I had bought to remember the trip. That bright but plain keychain looked extremely strange. For some reason, I stared at the glass of water he had been drinking the whole time. It was on the table, lit up by the lights in the room. The tremors from the bed shook the water. And while he was holding me down, he said, 'Your personality, the life you lived, not ever wanting to lose to anyone, everything you've ever done since you were born, it's like it was all just so someone could do this to you, isn't it?' He was on top of me, moving, and I was underneath him, crying. I thought I would go mad from how heartless he was. 'The moment I saw you, I imagined it ending like this. I'd been so excited for this moment.' I didn't understand. He didn't smile. He looked so serious. It was like he wanted to savor everything he was feeling during sex."

I didn't know what to say.

"When the sex was over, he looked at me strangely. It was like he was trying to tell why a hopeless woman who had just been raped still keeps breathing, still keeps existing. And then, when he looked at me, worn ragged, he felt my pain and started crying again. And then, gradually, he started to get excited. While he looked at me, I watched helplessly as his breathing grew wild again, right in front of my eyes. If he was still excited after sex, I had already guessed what he'd do to me next. I was so scared, I left the room. To be honest, I ran away."

She smiled slightly.

"That's why my life still isn't over. Didn't I make it through over ten years of working in some chauvinist company, out in the country? I found another job and I work in the afternoons. I will never feel that kind of sex again . . . But the wounds from having experienced that will never go away. There's a permanent dent inside me. He carved away something very important. Not my job or my hope or my happiness. No. Something more fundamental. He took that fundamental thing from me, savored it, and then threw it away. I may never be able to return to who I was. The wound of getting pleasure from what he did to me, pleasure so intense I didn't know what to do, that will never disappear. That's what it means to come into contact with a monster."

She looked at Shota, sleeping at the edge of the room.

"I don't know what happened to him after that, or what he's doing now. And I don't know if Shota was conceived that day in Tokyo, but he's his child. Time just passed and I didn't know what to do. Being the age I was, I felt a lot of pressure with that baby in my stomach. So I decided to have him. I had a C-section, so I don't really know if it hurt to give birth. But he's cute. I don't regret it. He's a good kid, don't you think?"

I nodded. Why had Eri told me all that? Maybe she trusted me. Maybe the wall that closed off her insides, that strength, had grown a little weak. Eri's body was worn down from alcohol. No one around her noticed her decline. Even though I was by her side, I couldn't do anything to help. One night when it was snowing, Eri left her room alone, as if something was calling her. She was drunk, and got hit by a car.

That night, I watched from my window as it snowed in Tokyo for the first time in ages. For some reason, the moon shone uncomfortably bright. Thin clouds stretched across the sky, but behind them, the moon gave off enough light to fill the sky.

—

THE INSECT OF a man in front of me was asleep, his chest rising and falling. In the garbage can was a balled-up magazine, and on the table, a can of beer and a tube of some kind of ointment. This was a stranger's hotel room. I put out my cigarette and took off the man's gown. I was lucky that he had taken off his clothes for me. I stripped him completely naked, flipped him facedown like a dog, and raised his hips. I tied his hands behind his back. I scattered the hotel's snacks around his face. Next I ripped a page out of the hotel notepad, wrote I LOVE RENHO, and stuck it on the man's naked back. I giggled while I took pictures of him. I didn't feel any heat in my body, but still I thought this was even better than the time with the anchor. Eri would probably have laughed if she saw this guy. Eri was always calm and cool, but she probably would have laughed. Shota would have laughed, too. I couldn't see the moon through the window, but I wished the moon could have seen, too. If the cruel moon had seen this, even it probably would have laughed a little.

4.

IT WAS A weekend night in Ikebukuro.

Every street was overflowing with people. The hanging neon words shone with purpose. All those lights collided, illuminating the city. I tried to use my whole body to feel the city at night as I walked down an alley on the west side of the station. There was a fire in the distance. A fire truck slipped by easily, its red ripping open even the clashing neon and stopping all the pedestrians and vehicles along its path. I could see gray smoke rising in the distance. Fires cause anxiety. The ensuing bustle, like a festival, raises the temperature of the night. The moon was in the sky. An ancient name for the moon is Luna, which is the origin of the English word "lunacy." In Japanese, the word for possession, "tsuki," is also said to have originated from "tsuki," the Japanese word for moon. The human's internal clock runs at twenty-five-hour intervals, and thus one of our days is closer to the 24.8 hours it takes the moon to revolve around the earth than the twenty-four hours it takes the earth to go around the sun. The revolution of the moon is always deviating from the earth's trek around sun. Humans are drawn less to the sun than the moon. They are drawn less to the day than the night. Less to the everyday than to quiet lunacy.

When I was a kid, I didn't want to be with anyone, so I would spend my afternoons in my room, and at night, I would quietly sneak out of the orphanage and gaze at the world outside. The moon was always there, a strange light, eternally suspended far, far away in the night sky. I didn't know anything back then, but I thoroughly researched everything I thought was somehow connected to me.

I entered a back alley, and the din of the night gradually grew quieter. I heard a voice ahead of me. In the entryway to a bar was a businessman yelling at a woman. I wasn't sure where she was from, but the woman getting yelled at was not Japanese. She was one of the foreign Asian women who stick out in these parts. The man yelling was drunk and animated. I wonder if he would yell like that if there was a big foreign man in front of him instead. He was screaming about how we do things in Japan. Stupid stuff. He spoke with discriminatory words. He was one of those cowardly people who look down on and denigrate others because they subconsciously wish to feel superior. The kind of person who's always trying to compensate for their own fragility. The man's suit was damp. He looked like trash. I approached him.

"The people in this organization are from overseas. You should cut it out."

"What?"

"These people, they really hate trouble . . . Wait. Don't you know where we are?"

Because of my lie, the round-faced man next to him

tried to stop the man who was yelling. He acted like he had no choice but to tone it down since someone else was stopping him. He lingered for a while, but eventually disappeared from the front of the bar. That kind of man could still go home and smile and hold his kids. He'd probably become a lay judge, talking the whole time about his sense of civic duty. To show that I hadn't interfered out of sympathy, I walked by the woman who had been yelled at without looking at her.

I looked up at the moon again. The moon kept shining. Its light looked wet. When ancient people watched the moon wax little by little, become full, and then finally wane, they saw in it the passage of their whole lives. Looking up at that unchanging cycle of waxing and waning, they came up with the concept of fate, the idea that the future is already decided. I don't believe in fate, and I don't really like fortune-telling.

I could see the tout, Kimura. He was a ways off, waving at me. He's loose with women, but he's worked as a go-between for me for a lot of jobs that couldn't be done in the open. I knew I could trust him with work. Back when I worked at the club, I asked him to introduce me to a black market doctor so I could get a coworker who was addicted to drugs into a hospital without her getting found out by the police. As long as I paid him properly, he kept all of his promises. I waved back at him. The light of the moon made everything behind him look slightly blue. The light was passing through a cloud of white exhaust.

I got a text message. It was from Hasegawa. Since I'd met with him, he had invited me to the orphanage three times, but I always made up an excuse and turned him down. I thought it would be all right to go, but what that man who took my knife had said held me back. I was sure he had mistaken Kondo for someone else, but somehow his words stuck with me. Something inside me, my intuition or something, couldn't ignore what he said.

As I went into an even deeper alley, the sounds of the city suddenly died out. Women stood along every dark road, their legs exposed. In Shinjuku there have been serious police crackdowns on prostitution, but there are still countless blind spots in this part of the city. In the appointed alley was a black luxury car. Coming to meet

Yata felt like such a bother. He could just tell me what to do by email, and then I wouldn't have to see him.

When I got in the car, it was even colder than outside. Like always, Yata was sitting up straight, but he looked a little tired.

"This man. Look at this picture. He's in room 205 at that hotel now. Say that Ami couldn't make it, so you went instead."

"If he asks why?"

"Say anything. It would probably sound more realistic if you say that she's got dermatitis instead of a cold or something. We don't need pictures this time. I want you to take his laptop."

"But he'll notice."

"That's fine. No, actually, that's better. It's a good opportunity to let this man know definitively that he is being targeted. But don't try to take it by force. That would be too obvious, and I want things to go smoothly."

I looked at the man in the photo. He had a plain face, but I got a bad feeling.

"Maybe I'm wrong, but haven't you been giving me a lot of work recently?"

"Huh?"

"The last assignment was a really tricky one. That corporate director."

"What are you talking about?"

"What?"

"I never asked you to do that."

My neck began to sweat. Yata looked straight at me. He was not joking.

"What are you saying? Didn't you email me asking me to do it? The last time we had a rush job, you sent me an email, too, right? It was from your address. The code to open the zipped files was also the same."

I logged into my email on my cell phone. I opened the messages from Yata and showed him the screen. Yata looked serious as he stared at the screen. The address was definitely his.

"I didn't send these."

"You didn't?"

"This is bad."

The car went silent. Yata leaned back and slowly pulled out a cigarette. He stared at the bottom of the steering wheel, thinking.

". . . What kind of man was the target?"

"I've still got a picture. I'll show you."

"I told you not to save any pictures."

"It was funny, so I put it on my phone. That's all. I'm sorry, but this time it turned out for the best, didn't it?"

I showed Yata the humiliating picture of that fat man. Yata's face grew even more stern, and he kept staring at the picture. Condensation formed on the windows.

". . . This is really bad."

"Do you know him?"

"That's not your concern . . . This is going to get really bad."

A group of drunk people walked by the window. They passed through the night, oblivious of what was happening in this car.

"But this wasn't my fault. Someone hacked your email account or something, right? And that means they know about me. I think I should be the one complaining."

"Be quiet," Yata said softly. I think that was the first time I had seen him so deep in thought. I can't imagine anyone else witnessing these small, secret acts of Yata's.

I didn't know what the work I did was being used for, or who was asking for these jobs to be done. I didn't know anything about Yata either, but he wasn't the type of guy to make this kind of mistake. That's why this case must have been so mysterious and grave to him. His reaction had nothing to do with me directly.

". . . We'll deal with this after. We don't have time. Go to the hotel."

"But . . ."

"There's one thing I need to tell you. The man at the hotel you're going to, he might not look like much, but you should be careful. He's a terribly violent man."

"Got it."

I looked at the picture again.

"Hurry up and go."

"You're not going to take me? Couldn't you have at least met me near the job, then?"

"I like it here."

Yata stared blankly ahead. Straight ahead several foreign women—I wasn't sure where they were from— were standing on the side of the road.

". . . There is a system to this world . . . That's why

I love it. I love staring at the people excluded from it. I love seeing the people tortured by this system."

". . . What?"

"Go."

Suddenly, Yata returned to his usual emotionless self. He opened the car door for me before I had the chance.

I RETURNED DOWN the road I had come and headed to the hotel. I looked once more at the man's picture. His hair was parted in the middle, and his face was completely plain. If he was actually going to be problematic, I couldn't just do things the way I always did. If he forced me down onto the bed, I wouldn't be able to stop him. I'm an expert with my stun gun, but there was no guaranteeing that I'd be able to move.

"Prostitutes" like me exist everywhere. There are many of us recorded in history. We become the lovers of important people in society to dig up information. We get them to have sex with us, and once they've grown comfortable around us, we put them to sleep and steal what we're told to, or we threaten to expose our relationships. Every man—at least every straight man—wants a beautiful woman. We take advantage of that weakness, sexual desire. We use our beauty to dull their judgment and achieve our aim. But most of the time that is impossible without giving them our bodies. Living like I do is hard. A while back, there was a story in the news about some women who pretended to sell their bodies, tricked men into S&M play, then tied them up and ran away with their wallets. I'm a lot like them. But it's only a matter of time until I can't get by just doing things my way.

My chest had started pounding a long time ago.

There was no time. I took the hotel's employee entrance and climbed the stairs. I caught my breath in front of the man's room and knocked on the door. Until I saw him, I wouldn't know what the best approach was. I knocked a second time, but there was still no response. The door was unlocked. I had heard stories about prostitutes who had let themselves into their clients' rooms and then the clients, without any discussion of what they were about to do, raped them. Those men probably wanted to commit a sex crime. I opened the door cautiously. I noticed I was smiling. My nerves were stretched to the breaking point. This was the feeling of confronting the sexual desires of an entirely unknown man. Those men who, regardless of their position in society, regardless of the lives they lived, regardless of everything, expose their true, hidden desires and try to take me with their whole bodies. I evade them, double-cross them, and escape from them. I make a mockery of them all. Whatever people want from me, whatever life demands from me, no matter who tries to catch me, I will escape and keep laughing at them all. I will live my life in this whirlpool of desire and betrayal. I will make them submit to me, while feeling the heat that comes from being desired. I will rise, feeling the even greater heat that comes from betraying someone. I will rise to a dark peak. That place is mine alone, and envied by no one. In that instant, I become my true self. I feel like I've been set free from everything. From those who try to control me. And from all the powers in this world that try to regulate my life. Those powers that push everyone along. There is a heat born within me when I fiercely defy whatever appears before my eyes. I had no intention of stopping myself from opening that door. My heart was pounding. I'd probably die soon.

The lights were on. I said "Excuse me," and stepped carefully into the room. What was he going to do? How was he going to try to fuck me?

I felt a sharp pain in my heart. My arms and legs lost their strength. I saw what was there, and my body responded, but I couldn't process what was in front of my eyes. The sheets on the bed were bulging, as if something were sealed inside. Blood leaked from the edges of the bulge. I approached it, unprepared for what I would see. My arms moved like it was their duty. The chill of the sheets traveled through my fingers. The roughness of those sheets felt strange to me. It also seemed strange that the light next to the bed wasn't on. I pulled back the sheet slowly. I could see the hair on his head. That raw blackness pierced something inside me. I couldn't breathe. I yanked back the sheet the rest of the way as if by reflex. There was a knife standing in the exact center of the man's chest. It was the man from the photo. His suitcase was open, and the contents were scattered around the room. My toes were touching the socks someone had tossed on the carpet. The computer I had come for was gone. I looked at the man once again, and saw that there was a strange look in his dead eyes. What was the last thing he had seen? Something inside me began falling down, down. I saw myself bursting out screaming, sitting down right there. The feelings had arrived late, but now they were chasing after me. I focused on steadying my legs. My pulse quickened further. I felt someone right behind me. It was still too early to scream. I slid my hand into my bag and gripped my lucky knife. I knew the stun gun would be of no use. I turned around fast, and just when I confirmed there was no one behind me, the phone rang, piercing the silence.

It was too loud. It ripped apart the atmosphere of the room. I took deep breaths and stared at the room's white phone. I thought about how there must be someone on the other end of the receiver. I wasn't sure if I should pick it up. But the sharpness of the sound demanded I answer quickly. I took control of my breathing, approached the phone, and picked it up as if I had no choice.

"You must be Yurika Kajima."

Sweat ran down my back. Kajima. That was my old last name. The last name that I had never told anyone. A name that even Yata probably didn't know.

"Your world is about to get interesting. Tell that to the man who sent you here."

There was a lot of noise on the other side of the receiver. I was confused. It felt like all that noise was surrounding me. I couldn't recognize this man's voice.

"That is, if you can get out of this hotel safely."

I put down the receiver and left the room. I ran to the storage closet at the end of the hall, opened the door cautiously, went in, and locked it behind me. The large shelves were lined neatly with white sheets and towels. I knew everything about this hotel. I could leave through this window and climb down the fire escape. I didn't know how to extend it, but I could figure it out. But the window wouldn't open. Surprised, I looked at the lock and saw that it was unbelievably rusted. My vision grew cloudy. I had to calm down. It wasn't like my life had been easy up until now. There was no reason for these people to take me lightly. No matter how many times I called Saito, he didn't answer. The window was moist with condensation. Should I break it? But if I did that, they'd know where I was from the sound.

I leaned on the wall, wondering if I was being toyed with. If they'd really planned on killing me, wouldn't they have done it in that room? They could have gotten me from behind while I was distracted by the corpse. Just like my premonition. There was no reason to call, and no reason to let me out of that room.

I opened the door and went into the hallway. I could see my breath. Just in case, I gripped the knife in my bag. It has always kept me safe just by being there. Lifeless rectangular doors lined both sides of the hallway. The air was freezing. Those doors seemed to express the hallway's will to maintain the silence. I walked quietly past that succession of rectangles. If I took the elevator, there'd be nowhere to run, so I took the emergency exit to be safe. For some reason, the railing was wet. Just as I thought, no one was there. I got out of the hotel.

Out of curiosity, I went back in the hotel. The hands peeking through the space at the front weren't Saito's. But he worked at this time every day. I went outside.

I had called Saito, but he'd never picked up. What was I supposed to do now? I didn't know Yata's number, so I couldn't call him.

THE NEXT DAY, Yata told me to meet him. He said he knew everything, and he asked me to come so we could fix it. Yata showed me a single photo. It was a tall man wearing sunglasses and smiling faintly as he walked. "I want you to approach him and take something," he said.

"What kind of guy is he?"

"He works behind the scenes of everything. Many people have died because of him. He's one of those extraordinary individuals who make things happen. He has many names. Nerigami. Yoshihara. Kizaki."

My heart dropped. Kizaki. That's what the man who took my knife had called Kondo. But would that mean Kondo didn't actually work at the orphanage? The picture wasn't clear, and I couldn't tell if that man was Kondo. But what did this mean? What was this?

I couldn't understand. For some reason, the moonlight overhead was growing stronger.

5.

I HAD A dream.

I was sitting in the middle of a field of grass wet with rain.

When I felt the presence of the moon, I noticed that there was a red book of paintings in my hands. When I was young, I admired the depictions of Phryne in that book. Her body was so beautiful and white. I wanted that body. I stared at the book. I thought that a woman could laugh away this world. In ancient Greece, she lived free, even though she was a prostitute. When she was called to court and charged as a criminal, she showed the men her body. They fell for her, and let her go free of any charges. It was thought that a woman that beautiful must have been a priestess of the goddess Aphrodite. Strong people are free. But I lived in other people's houses, and wore other people's clothes. Being like her was just a distant dream.

The pictures in my hands got wet and began to fall apart. I tried to gather up the scraps, but the wet paper crumbled and melted into my surroundings. For some reason, when I felt the moonlight, the clouds grew lower. They kept getting lower, like they were falling. I walked. My body got wet from the grass.

I began to feel the gravity of the moon growing stronger in the distance. The moon shone eerily. Excited, it used its gravity to make wild distant seas. Creatures clamored in the darkness. The sea raged on, and the moon overflowed, letting out even more light. For some reason, the clamoring of that light shook something inside me without making the slightest noise. I tried to collect the ravaged bits of Phryne. The night is a raging festival, an enormous ocean pulsing with waves. That light was too strong. It hurt. I wasn't sure if it was good or evil.

I WASN'T SURE where I was when I woke up. My body was moist with sweat. I remembered I was in a hotel, and got up.

I couldn't go home after what happened. Besides, there was nothing there I had to go back to get. I could buy clothes, and there was nothing personal saved on my computer. Everything was on the hard drive in my bag. I always carry what I need with me. Why? I stared at my bag.

I turned on the TV, but the incident hadn't made the news.

I stared at Kizaki's picture on the table and thought about my most recent exchange with Yata. He was exhausted. His face had been so plain, but now he looked a bit thin, and his eyes and cheeks were dark with stress.

"If he's really so powerful, I want you to become his woman."

Absentmindedly, I watched Yata's white cigarette smoke.

"Then you can share his information with us, and take what we need from him."

"No thanks."

"I thought you'd say that."

We were in the usual alley. As always, women lined the road.

"We're not threatening you into doing this work. You're doing it of your own accord. I'd like you to use your body to do this job. You always refuse to use your body on a job, but you get better results than the women who do. You're smart. You have to be to work as a prostitute who doesn't sell her body. You're efficient, and you don't make too much trouble for the men involved. So I haven't said anything about the way you do things. Your clients think you just put them to sleep and take their money. You and I both know that's not all you do. And as long as the results are the same, you can do whatever you want."

Yata took a small breath.

"But this time, it would be best if you became his woman. There are plenty of women I could ask, but I think you're the most suitable for the job. The problem is, no matter how much I research you, I can't find any weak point."

I made a sullen face to hide the fact that I was shaken up.

"To make someone do something, you can either use temptation or threats. You have no weak points to threaten. We can't find anyone precious to you. Anyone you feel the need to protect. You're not even that attached to your own life. Even if I say I'll kill you if you don't do it, you'll just refuse and run away."

I thought of Eri and Shota's faces. I looked at a distant building and lit a cigarette.

"My network is huge. If you tried to get away from me, we would capture you, and depending on the circumstances, we might really kill you. But we don't get anything out of that. You're smart. We wouldn't catch you easily. You would seduce my people, use them, and keep running. We would have to spend a lot of money and man power on you. We'd go through tremendous pains to kill you, but there'd be nothing in it for us. I don't bear grudges. I don't have strong emotions like that. Given the costs required to kill you, it just wouldn't be logical. So, I'll give conditions you'll agree to. I won't say become his woman. Do what you always do. And just take something from him."

". . . What are you?"

"I told you in the beginning, it's better not to ask. To know is to get involved. And getting involved only increases the chance that we will have to kill you if you ever betray us."

A skinny woman who had been standing in front of us found a customer. They linked arms and went into a building. I thought her smile was not one of happiness but of relief.

"And if I still say no?"

"We have no choice. We'll compromise. Though there's no value in it for us, we'll have to kill you."

My eyes met Yata's. I could see touches of anxiousness in his small eyes. My throat went dry. When did I get myself into this situation?

"What do I take?"

"Any information this man has. We need to analyze it and figure out his goals and plans. We don't know his background. He has no family history."

"What does that mean?"

"We're not sure. Given the number of security guards he has, we can't take anything from him by force. We're not sure if he owns a home. Our only options are to have someone pickpocket him on the street, or get a girl to take things secretly. The only time a man like this is alone, aside from when he's in the bathroom, is when he's sleeping with a woman."

I kept looking at the man in the photo. My heartbeat quickened, and I began to sweat.

"I probably don't have to say this, but there are others besides you. We're investigating this man from every angle. You're just one of many. Your reward will be determined by the quality of the information you bring."

I have no weak points. Yata's words stuck with me. That's not strength, though. It shows a certain separation from life. It's closer to loneliness or despair.

I TOOK A shower, sat on the sofa, and lit a cigarette. I wondered if I didn't feel hungry because I was nervous. All of my weaknesses have vanished from this world. It's been one year since Shota died.

At first it was just a fever. Eri had died, and Shota was sent to an orphanage. The same one that Hasegawa and I belonged to. Shota was just seven, and he was a beautiful child, so everyone expected him to find foster parents right away. But he was a cold child, and also weak. He mostly just lay in bed at the orphanage all day. Maybe it was because he'd known me since he was a baby, but he'd talk to me a little when I visited. He was still unfriendly, though. And I didn't know how to approach these things called "children."

"Aren't you going to give me something?"

"Don't be such a baby. I just gave you some candy the other day."

That day, his fever hadn't gone down like normal. He was diagnosed as having some kind of virus and was taken to the hospital. But once there, it became hard for him to breathe, and all of a sudden he was hooked up to some kind of respirator. Though the cause of his illness was still unknown, the doctors suddenly said he only had a few days left to live. They said it was either a rare disease or a congenital disorder, and the people at the orphanage grew scared. They wondered if they had the money to pay for special medical treatments. Only good people worked at the orphanage, but their judgment was clouded by the suddenness of events.

I said I'd pay for everything and that I wanted them to test him thoroughly and treat him as best as they could. It wasn't because of goodwill toward Shota or because I felt I had to fulfill some obligation to Eri. I said that because of this rebellious streak I have. Even I can't explain it clearly. A kid from the orphanage was going to die without explanation, and all the people around him were completely useless. He was hooked into a respirator, but still his tiny hands struggled. I wanted to cheat fate, or whatever it was trying to claim this child. The doctor said that in Shota's state, it would be difficult to do tests as they would put his life in danger, but I continued to speak my mind. I had to defy them. I couldn't let him die this way.

Shota was moved to a university hospital where they discovered he had several conditions. I listened to many unfamiliar words. ST-T segment abnormality, BNP, spironolactone, ACE inhibitor, beta blockers. I was told that of all of his ailments, his heart was in the gravest state. When they said that he would probably need a transplant overseas, the people from the orphanage pulled back yet again. They really didn't have that kind of money. They tried to raise money, but they couldn't get much. It wasn't because of the cruelty or indifference of the public. People can be cruel, but they can also be just as kind. It was really a problem of the way the people at the orphanage approached the public. The fundraising for another transplant in the neighboring prefecture had attracted a lot of support, and they got the money they needed.

I didn't say I would give money out of kindness. I didn't have anything to protect, or any hope for life. It's no big deal what becomes of the bank balance of someone like me. But I gave everything I had, and it still wasn't enough. I met Yata just when I was wondering where I could borrow money. I worked at an expensive club, and he came in looking for someone to do some strange work. He looked just like an ordinary man, but there was no lust in his eyes. Instead, he looked at the girls like he was searching for the right one. His timing was so perfect, it felt creepy, and when I asked him about it later, he told me he only brought up work after investigating me thoroughly. Really, there's nothing you need to watch out for more than people who approach you when you're in a tough situation.

"Three hundred thousand yen for one job. If that goes well, the next one will be five hundred thousand."

My job was to create weak points in the lives of people who were prominent in society. Photos and videos of us entering hotels together. Proof of men fooling around naked with a prostitute in bed. Proof of the shame of sex. Proof of things no one wants known about them. If I did it twenty times, I'd make at least a hundred million yen. I needed as much money as I could get.

"You can move people with either temptation or threats, but threats work best. The higher their position, the better it works. We don't say anything crude, like we're going to put these pictures everywhere if you don't listen to us."

That first time, Yata called just me to the VIP room at the club. He didn't touch my shoulders or legs. He just explained everything quietly.

"We choose people we want to use, and manually we

create weak points in their lives. It has been going on in this world through all of history."

I remembered the phone call his subordinate made to someone a few days before. He was on his cell phone, laughing, and when he seemed like he was about to hang up, the person he was talking to brought up something unexpected and the tone of the conversation changed. That young man never used a single threatening word.

"Yes, that's right. Well, it would be great if that wasn't true . . . You haven't been threatened recently, have you?"

After saying that, he switched the phone to his left hand, and brought his glass to his lips.

"A strange man was following you around? . . . Ah, he was trying to get information on you? . . . He's a small fry. They're everywhere. Hm? . . . Oh, you went to a hotel in Ikebukuro recently? Ah, that kind of place. That time. I see . . . Did you sleep there?"

That man smiled that whole time.

"Yes. Oh, really? To your place? No, we're not sure of the details ourselves . . . That's really worrisome. No, I heard they're selling them in pretty awful channels . . . If they're fake, I don't think it matters. Oh, if that's the case . . . I see . . . Well, we'll do what we can . . . Like I said, if they got out it would be quite a scandal . . . You'd be laughed at by everyone . . . You have to worry about your wife and kids, too . . . Yes, for a person like you . . . Yes, it's fine. They're small fries anyway, so it'll be easy . . . Ha ha ha, we won't do anything criminal. Don't worry . . . Yes, it won't take too much . . . How should I say, it's out of the kindness of our hearts. We just want to be of help to you . . . Well, we're asking so much of you right now . . . Yes, if you would help us out as well, we'd much appreciate it . . . Ha ha, we should meet soon . . . It will be fine . . . We would never use your photo or videos for anything bad . . . We'll dispose of them right away . . . Yes, immediately."

I wasn't sure what kind of conversation that was at the time. As I recalled that conversation, I stared at Yata.

"And the important thing—"

He and I were the only ones in that huge VIP room, and he just kept talking. When I think about it, I was probably purposefully made to listen to the subordinate's conversation.

"—is to stop after one time. The more you do this

kind of thing, the more likely it gets that the target won't listen and the photos will go public. But we achieve our goals with just that one exchange."

Yata stared at me with unmoving eyes.

"What are you people?"

"There's no need to say."

Yata lit a cigarette. They were thin menthols, like women smoke. The white strips of smoke blurred Yata's expression.

"This world has a fundamental structure. The wealthy stay wealthy. The haves continue to have. That is the structure. There are entrances into that structure. But that kind of system has been created in every country. And not just one in each country. They're all interlocked. They form a supple, flexible system."

". . . What?"

"We maintain that system. When something occurs that seems dangerous to us, we guide people's thoughts with delicate instruction, bring down people dangerous to us, or, depending on the situation, we join forces with them. And that's not all we do. To keep everything run-ning smoothly at critical moments, we must sometimes take action, like we're doing now. But, to me it's just a kind of hobby."

I thought his plain face, and plain suit, and plain shoes were disgusting. The humidifier in the VIP room kept spitting out white steam. For some reason, my surroundings grew blurry. But I had no time to think.

BECAUSE SHOTA'S ILLNESS was classified as rare, we received some money for treatment from the government, and though the expense of his transplant overseas did not qualify for assistance and was terribly expensive, the orphanage also collected money little by little. After receiving appropriate treatment, Shota recovered a little. And after regaining his life, he really was beautiful.

Lying in bed in the hospital he told me, "Machines are amazing." He was talking about his diagnostic machine. "That house was old. But my machine is cool. Money and stuff . . . It's a lot of trouble. Isn't it?"

I wondered if his right cheek was itchy. It was always a bit red.

"You shouldn't worry about it. No one's worried about

the money. We're getting some from insurance, and I'll pay the rest."

"Why?"

"Because I'm rich. There's no reason for anyone to worry about it."

Shota was still grumpy and didn't listen to what anyone said, so he wasn't very popular with the nurses. Even though the curtains in his room were always open and the scenery outside was beautiful, he just stared at the ceiling for some reason. I'm not sure what he spent all his time thinking about.

I did the jobs I was given one by one. I seduced men and betrayed them. I had the skills. But those skills would never bring me happiness.

He hadn't gotten the transplant yet, but after surgery Shota started growing a bit healthier. He even made it to the hospital garden occasionally. He would choose times after the sun had set, when no one was there. He would take off his slippers and put on sneakers. They were small, but they were proper blue sneakers, with laces and all. He would hang his feet off the side of the bed and stare at those shoes he put on himself while I tied them tight.

At first, his legs were weak, so he had to hold my hand while he walked, but eventually he could walk on his own. He never would get in a wheelchair.

"What's this?" he asked. He had gone up to a flower, and turned around to face me.

"It's a flower."

"But what kind of flower?"

When I think back, it was a morning-star lily. But that knowledge I acquired as a child had gone missing.

"Let's call it . . . Barry."

"Let's call it what?"

"It's a pretty flower . . . There was this woman named du Barry. She went from being a prostitute to dating the king of France, and even got to move into the palace."

Shota looked at me worried. "What! What about this flower?"

"That one's pretty too, so let's call it Phryne. It's white, after all."

"What?"

"Phryne was an ancient prostitute. She was really rich, and she even had people make a statue of her and put it next to the statues of all the rulers of Greece. Isn't that amazing?"

"I don't know."

The hospital was surrounded by small hills, but in the garden, it was the hospital building itself that rose up and surrounded us. You couldn't see outside at all. There was a siren blaring in the distance.

"Hey." After a long silence, Shota suddenly looked up at me. "You're not really rich, are you? Can I really get all these surgeries?"

A dim white light shone on Shota's thin shoulders. For some reason, the walls of the hospital and stone tile covering the ground stood out to me. I felt irritated at myself, maybe for still letting his comment get to me.

"Don't worry about it. It's fine."

"Why?"

"Why? . . . Oh, you have to marry me. To pay me back."

Shota looked at me for a moment. His face looked so serious, and he nodded. It was like he was accepting that as his responsibility for being saved. Even though his life had not yet started, he took on his first responsibility with resolution. I was overcome by some inexplicable emotion, and before I knew it, I was holding Shota.

"I'm just kidding. Love whoever you want. I . . ."

When I think back, the words I told him were ones that, even now, I have never been told.

"You're important. I need you, so I'll do anything I can for you. I was there when you came into this world. I said, hello, little boy. I know I'm not much, but I was there for you. You're always a sourpuss, and aren't cute at all, but that doesn't matter. I don't care what other people think. I love you."

Shota looked at me, serious. I was a bit shocked at what I said. I got this feeling that I would have to do a better job keeping myself together.

"But I guess I will make you marry me. Just 'cause you're cool."

I smiled, and the edges of Shota's mouth moved slightly. When I think about it now, that must have been a smile. He'd had to watch as his mom gradually ruined herself with alcohol. I wonder if he ever smiled then. He reached his arm out slowly toward my hand. We held hands and walked back.

But Shota never made his transplant. I was informed that his condition had suddenly gotten worse. I rushed over to the hospital, but by the time I got there his eyes were closed. I will always remember the grimace on his face. It was like all the unfairness of this world had been taken on by his small body, and that grimace was the scar it left. Seeing him like that crushed our hopes and all that we had prepared for emotionally. There was no changing it. Reality was too sudden, too undependable. I could see the moon through the window. I forgot to glare at that incomprehensible light. Standing there, I couldn't even cry. Tears finally came a few days later when I saw a small, thin child trying to get on his bike in a parking lot. I don't know why I cried then. I was standing on a narrow road, and I couldn't hold the tears back. I thought they would flow forever. I was powerless. It was like all I could do was cry.

All of the money we collected for the transplant we gave to kids in situations similar to Shota's. On the inside, the crushed feeling never got better. The image of Shota's furrowed brow never disappeared from the back of my mind.

I kept taking jobs from Yata. After Shota's passing, I couldn't grow attached to anything. I couldn't make sense of his death. But the days passed. Whatever my situation, time just passes, unconcerned.

I lost all of my weaknesses. Without hope, there's also no need to endure the cruel sadness of losing someone. All that's left is a pathetic life like mine.

6.

SEVERAL LEATHER COUCHES lined the big room. In the middle was a huge table covered with alcohol and food. Next to every man sat a woman in a dress. There were about fifteen or sixteen men there, and more than twice as many women. Unlike a normal party, the room was pretty dark. Spread across the floor was a rug with a strange pattern made of many lines intersecting in a complicated fashion. We were on the thirty-first floor of the Reldurant Hotel.

The men spoke quietly, and the women by their sides nodded along. Every woman's appearance was highly polished. I showed someone the card Yata gave me. All that was printed on it was a complicated color pattern. I pretended to have been sent here and snuck in. I needed to listen to all the demands of any man here. When I first came in, a strange man who seemed to be managing the party told me that. I didn't know the backgrounds of any of the men there, but they were all wearing expensive clothes. They must not have been starving for women, either. None even tried to touch the girls sitting next to them.

In the corner, sitting on an enormous sofa, was Kizaki. He was wearing sunglasses even though it was dark. Silent women surrounded him while he talked to an Arab-looking man sitting across from him. Even though he was far away, I knew it was him immediatey. I took a glass of champagne in my hand, smiled, and approached him slowly. Violent noises rose up from deep in my chest. I was trying something desperate now.

EVEN AFTER LOOKING at his photo, and even seeing him here in person in the dark, I could not tell if he was really Kondo. But after hearing the name Kizaki from that man who took my knife, I felt there was a possibility that they were the same person, even if they seemed to have a different feel to them. And, when I considered all the circumstances and the timing of Yata's request, there was also a chance that this man was involved with the hacking of Yata's email, me getting sent on a job I wasn't supposed to have, the dead body in the hotel, and that phone call where someone mentioned my old last name. And if that man really was Kondo, I still wouldn't know why he was trying to approach me, but it would mean he had some business with me, and that he knew what I do.

I couldn't tell Yata that this man might know who I was. If I said that, Yata would try to use it against me, and I would get dragged in even deeper.

Now I had to face this man who might know all my tricks, and I had to steal something of his. I don't consider myself particularly attached to my life, but I don't want to die a violent death. I needed to get past this and convince Yata I did my job. Suddenly, I noticed the heat in my body. Something began moving inside me— as if I were being sucked toward something. I exhaled. I was nervous, but being nervous wasn't an option. There were only a few ways to take advantage of the fact that Kizaki knew who I was, and get out of this place.

Carefully arranging my short dress and my bare legs, I sat in the empty space next to the Arab man across from Kizaki. When I turned my eyes to Kizaki, my heart began to race. His shoulders were wide, he was tall, and there was something forceful about his body. The Arab next to me smiled and raised his glass slightly. Kizaki stared straight at me.

"... I see."

Kizaki kept staring at me.

"Do you know why all of the women in Marquis de Sade's books are unhappy?" he asked suddenly after producing a slight smile. Judging from his expression and his voice, he was definitely Kondo. But would I have recognized him so quickly in this darkness if no one had mentioned it to me before? He really had nothing to do with the orphanage. But I had no idea what that meant.

He knew who I was, but he didn't change his expression at all when he saw me. I pretended not to know who he was either, smiled calmly, and stared back at him. My pulse grew faster.

"Because they're beautiful. When beautiful women are granted a chance at happiness, they're also granted a chance to fall into despair. And the closer they get to whatever they desire, the more chances they're given to fail. You should remember that."

"Are you complimenting me?" I asked.

His expression would not budge. He hid behind his sunglasses, smiling. The woman next to him inched closer, and asked, "What about me?" She was tall and beautiful. But Kizaki did not even look at her. He just kept staring at me.

"I'm not complimenting you. Despair has greater gravity than happiness. That's how this world is." He continued to ignore the woman next to him and stare at me. Somehow, my pulse got even faster.

"I was just talking to this man about this earlier. Do you know about Gnosticism?"

"What's that?"

"It was the largest heretic faith, born during the early Christian era. Gnostics thought this world was created by a low-level god."

What was he talking about? I couldn't guess where this would lead.

"If you look around, humans plagued by disasters and illness, poverty and starvation, they fill the wilds of this world. The Gnostics thought it impossible that a good, all-powerful god created such an imperfect world. They concluded that the god that created this world must have been low-ranking amongst all the gods and filled with evil. As the Gnostics carried their children dying of starvation through the wilds, they looked up at the sky and cursed god. They stopped worshipping the god written about in the Bible. There were other, real gods out there. They thought they had to worship a better god, a god who had nothing to do with the creation of this world, and nothing to do with humans. This thinking is similar to a pattern you can see at orphanages, where suffering children cling to the hope that they alone have real parents, even though none of the children around them do."

Kizaki kept staring at me. I didn't change my expression.

"Practitioners of this heretical faith were persecuted by orthodox Christians, and disappeared from the main stage. There were many different groups. You must know about Cain. The man who, in legend, was the son of the first humans, Adam and Eve, committed the world's first murder by killing his brother, Abel. Among the Gnostics, there were even people who worshipped Cain. Their group was called the Canaanites. They thought that by disobeying an evil god, Cain did something good. They tried to do everything that was forbidden by God. They stole, and were very free with their sexuality. It must have been quite fun."

The Arab next to him jokingly gestured like he was apologizing to God.

"This man," Kizaki said, pointing at the Arab, "says I'm a Canaanite. That's a big mistake. I don't pray like that to anything. If I had to say, I sympathize with that poor god. Think about it. Don't you think it would be wonderful? You could see people writhing in pain and suffering right under your nose, and even savor *the movements of the feelings* born within them. And, at the same time, you could watch their admirable acts. You could feed on their depression, twisted by all the pain, feed on their positive feelings, and mix the two opposing emotions together within yourself. That god writhed for thousands of years, intoxicated. The world twists like a whirlpool, propelled by the countless dynamisms of those two opposite emotions. Where that leads is a mystery of course. But if the god who created this world was really a perfectly good being, would he, for example, make a world where animals have to eat animals to survive?"

Kizaki moved his hand slightly.

"Let's say there is a man on the bed in a love hotel in Ikebukuro, and you stab him straight through the chest."

I focused on my nerves and maintained my smile. I'm sure he was saying it on purpose, but he didn't show it at all.

"Just staring cruelly at that man as he suffers from his wound is boring. Smiling while you watch him suffer, that's boring, too. *You must feel what he feels.* Make your imagination call up his lover, and the parents who raised him, and shed tears of sympathy. But keep stabbing. Deeper. Deeper. Then, both the overwhelming, cruel joy of destroying a life and the warm feeling of sympathizing with that life will seep through you. When those two opposing feelings mix together and finally become one, human emotion will surpass the human. Good and bad will continue to provoke each other, those feelings will go beyond human capacity and keep rising up forever. Like a whirlpool. What's important is to *leave nothing unappreciated*. It's great. That moment."

Kizaki reached out and suddenly grabbed the neck of the woman next to him. He squeezed it tightly. She was surprised, and her eyes popped wide open. Kizaki's fingers sunk into her white, rubbery neck. She couldn't understand what was happening, but she felt the sheer strength of that hand. She wondered if she would actually die there, and startled by the sudden unfairness of life, her eyes, bursting with surprise, met mine. Five seconds passed as Kizaki continued to strangle her. Ten seconds. I kept up my smile, but it got hard to breathe. The air was tense, stinging. More time passed, and more time. Kizaki suddenly pulled back his hand,

and the woman collapsed, coughing. Kizaki smiled, his breathing not the slightest bit upset.

"Even at times like this, I think of others' emotions. I feel what it's like to be surprised, to have your life up to this moment ignored and to suddenly die for no reason . . . Do you see?"

I didn't change my expression. My life until now was not easy enough to let myself be bothered by something like this. I didn't know if the Arab sitting next to me understood what Kizaki was saying, but he was smiling.

"You're a scary man."

"Ha ha. You're funny. Tell me about yourself."

"Hm?"

"Introduce yourself."

"My name is Yurika."

I didn't see the point in lying.

"That's not what I mean. I want to know about your nature. Tell me about how you were born, what you've done in this world until now, and what you haven't done. Then I can grasp what you are, your nature, and what sort of tendencies you have. That is what I like. I like taking people in."

Kizaki kept staring at me. My pulse was racing, and I felt heat in my body. Things were happening fast.

"I can't do that. Not here, with all of these people."

I forced my eyes to tear up, and smiled at Kizaki sweetly, challenging him. Kizaki stood up and grabbed my arm. I took his arm and leaned my body against his as he started walking. What did this man intend to do with the woman who came to trap him? It got cold around me.

7.

I WALKED DOWN a dim hallway with Kizaki gripping my arm. Even when I tried to catch up to him, he managed to casually stay a bit ahead of me. My small bag felt heavy. His shoulders were wide. There wasn't a single wrinkle in his fine suit.

I didn't see any men who looked like bodyguards. It was just the two of us walking down the hallway. I could possibly accomplish my goal right now if I hit his exposed neck with my stun gun. But I couldn't move my arm. He pulled me along, his coercive force confusing my every movement. I felt with my whole body that something bad would happen if I made a move now.

When we reached the end of the hall, my pulse grew even wilder. He slowly opened a door, and on the other side were several men. The moment I tried to steady my body to run away, the men turned their backs to us and I noticed they were looking at something deep in the darkness of the room. A single spot was lit starkly, and I could hear a woman wailing. On a white platform lay a naked woman.

"It's a show. Watch."

She was tall, and her body was well balanced, and pale. She was beautiful. Her hands and arms were bound, and some sort of machine was attached to her genitals. She was on display in front of all those men, lit by an evil light. Her naked body was wet with sweat. She wailed and shook, but she could not move her bound arms and legs. She whispered something, raised her body for a second, and began shaking violently. She yelled again. The men smiled and stared at the woman as if they despised her. She looked less like she hated them than that she knew they hated her, and the more they hated her, the greater her desire. She cried and wailed. Her body kept responding to the machine. A woman crying but feeling pleasure is an ugly sight. I stared at her with hate as well. She had a terribly sexy body that must have enticed every man. Ejaculate squirted out of her and stuck to the suits of several of the men watching. They continued to smile, but looked as though wiping that liquid off was an awful chore. I felt myself fill with hate, but my body grew hotter and hotter.

"How depraved."

"You should keep watching."

A man in black quietly approached the woman. That man raised a lever on the apparatus, and the woman's wails grew louder. The man crouched by her, and brought his mouth close to her ear. Then he said, "Curse the world!"

"Ahhh! Ahhh!"

She opened her eyes and stared at the ceiling.

"Curse it!"

"I . . ."

The man lifted the handle even further.

"I . . . I want them to die! Die!"

"Who?"

"Everyone! Everyone, die!"

The woman screamed suddenly. The men continued to smile, and a quiet rustling passed through them. The room was filled with their cigarette smoke.

"Everyone. Everyone die! I'm the best. Everyone."

"What's wrong?"

"My father."

The woman writhed, and cried out. She looked as if she was gradually forgetting herself.

"What did your father do?"

"Ahhh! Ahhh! Dad. He . . . me . . ."

The men watching cheered quietly.

"And?"

"That's why. I . . . I killed him."

The men seemed satisfied, and another rustling ran through them.

"But it won't get better."

"That's right. It won't get better. You won't get better. That's why. More. More."

The woman screamed. When the man raised the handle again, she screamed, "More." The men watching grew gradually quieter.

"More! Give me more!"

The man furrowed his brow. The white smoke grew thicker. The man lifted the handle even further, and the woman began to laugh as if she had gone mad.

"Ha ha ha ha ha."

A stern look spread across the man's face. The men watching did not say anything. The woman's mouth was open wide.

"Cowards! Ha ha ha. Ahhh! More! Ahhh! Please. Ahhh! Die! Die! More!"

The way she pled so earnestly and desperately despite being tortured pricked something inside me.

"I beg you! Ahhh! It's not enough! Please!"

The men continued to watch, silent.

"Who do you think is in control here?" Kizaki asked suddenly, standing next to me. I was slightly surprised to hear his voice.

"The woman is."

"That's right."

The woman bent her back even further, and continued to plea.

"Masochism stimulates the other's desires, awakens the madness inside them, and drags it out. After that, you can keep begging for more and more. When the master isn't useful any more, the masochist can just change masters. The ultimate end of sadism is ruin and murder. The one in control is always the masochist."

The woman's body trembled and she continued yelling at the man.

"But there's no choice but to kill a monster like that," Kizaki said.

One of the men watching approached the woman silently and raised the handle as far as it could go. The woman let out a deep cry, and suddenly stopped moving. She was still breathing. She must have passed out.

"What a wonderful self-introduction. Don't you think?"

Kizaki was next to me, smiling.

"Maybe it was."

"You're next in this room."

I felt a chill run down my back, but I didn't let it show on my face and steadied my body.

"I can't say what I really think unless I'm alone with someone."

"Well, that's fine. Come. You should tell me everything about yourself. Tell me about the essence of your being."

He grabbed my arm again. He was strong. His movements were casual. We passed through the hallway and reached a bridge connecting the building to another. His room was probably at the end of this hall. I could see the moon through the windows of the bridge. It was huge. I noticed that my body was disgustingly hot. My plan probably wouldn't work. But I had no choice but to try. I couldn't shake his arm off. I had come this far. I couldn't run away.

For some reason the moon looked tinted red through the window. I tried to face the moon and make myself smile. The moonlight was strong. Strong enough to shake me. There was something painfully nostalgic about the red of the moon. "I'll show you." To give myself strength, I whispered to the moon in my head, "I'll show you my madness."

8.

EVEN AFTER ENTERING the room, Kizaki didn't turn on many lights. A single orange light shone in the darkness, casting his twisted shadow on the wall. In the large room was an illuminated aquarium, several shiny sofas arranged around a large table, and racks filled with wine and whiskey. The partitions separating his bedroom were opened. In the corner of that room was an enormous bed, and on top of his desk was a simple laptop computer. That was the first thing I laid my eyes on. From the windows of this top-floor apartment, I could see the lights of the surrounding buildings.

"Would you like something to drink?" I asked, shifting so my dress draped more revealingly over my chest. He sat on the sofa and lit a cigarette.

I put my bag down, chose a bottle of whiskey from the rack, and put ice in two glasses. The shelf was in the shadows, and he couldn't see what I was doing. Just in case, I positioned myself to make a blind spot. I twisted my ring so the fake gem faced down. I lifted the cap and dumped powder in the drink. My fingers were used to this movement as I had done it countless times. I poured the whiskey, added ice and mineral water, and approached the table with the two glasses in my hands. I passed one glass to Kizaki, and took the drugged one as my own.

"Excuse me."

I made a point to leave my seat. I turned my back to him and grabbed a towel to wipe off the drops of water stuck to the glasses. No one would drink the alcohol poured by a woman who's after you. He would change his glass for mine. I smiled, returned to the table, and stared at the glasses. They weren't switched. My pulse sped up slightly. The drugged drink was there on my side, and Kizaki was calmly drinking the whiskey I'd handed him.

"What's wrong?"

Kizaki smiled and glanced at me. I smiled as well, brought the glass to my lips, and took it away without drinking anything.

"May I sit next to you?" Without waiting for his reply, I took my glass and sat next to him. I pressed my shoulder against his, and showed him my drink.

"I made it too strong. Do you want this one?"

"You should make another."

"You're right."

I smiled slightly, and took his arm.

"Won't you hold me?"

I tried to look past his glasses into his eyes, and made a slightly embarrassed face. I leaned my body forward, crumpling the fabric around my legs and chest.

"I thought you would knock me down the second we entered the room."

"I'm not desperate for women," Kizaki said quietly. "I've slept with enough women to ruin it. I don't always enjoy regular sex."

"What kind of sex do you like?" I pressed my chest against his arm. "If you don't sleep with me, the manager will get mad. But I'm glad I'm with you. Fuck me."

I brought my face up close to his. I smiled at him challengingly.

"Or, are you scared of me? Scared of fucking me? Try to dominate me."

Kizaki kept staring.

"If that's how it is, I'll start things. It's all right as long as I get you excited, right?"

I kissed his neck, and wrapped my arm around him. My heart was beating like crazy, and I could feel the heat. I fingered the bracelet on the arm I put around him. I wondered if it would work. My metal bracelet was strangely shaped. It was said that during the cold war bracelets like this were used for assassinations. Yata had given it to me, and it sparkled beautifully. I gradually brought my arm up behind the back of his neck. I pushed on the bracelet's clip, and a needle popped out. In it was a type of nerve poison. It would paralyze someone, but not kill them. That was what Yata had said, but would it really work? The needle was shiny, extremely thin and sharp. The beauty of that needle took my breath away. I imagined that needle piercing the beautiful neck of a strong man. My hands did not shake. I focused on my nerves, grew obsessed with that beauty, and while running my lips along Kizaki's ears, brought the needle closer.

"All this metal gets in the way." Kizaki didn't move an inch. He just spoke quietly.

My hand stopped. I couldn't move.

"Metal gets in the way of sex. Take it off."

He smiled and looked at me. I smiled back. Our eyes were locked and a few seconds passed. Nervous, I put the needle away and took off my bracelet.

"I'm sorry about that."

I put the bracelet in my dress pocket. I made sure to keep up my smile.

"But it's beautiful. Show it to me."

Kizaki never stopped smiling. I began to lose my strength.

"Never mind that. Let's keep going." I took his arm.

"Just show it to me."

The room grew quiet. If you listened closely, you could hear the heater crying out in the background.

I couldn't decide what to do. Depending on what I did next, my life could end in a matter of seconds. For some reason, my body was hot. What would it feel like to die? Maybe in a second, without knowing anything, you just become nothing. My heart kept beating unreasonably, as if to resist the end I was approaching, as if to assert my life. I pulled my body away from Kizaki, and put the bracelet on the table. Then I sat on the sofa across from him.

"It doesn't really suit me."

I lost all my strength. Kizaki picked the bracelet up with his fingers.

"I was hired to come here. By a man called Yata." I looked at him, completely powerless. "At first I was doing it for money. But I got in too deep, and now if I don't do what he says, he'll kill me. I was sent here to try and figure out your plans. I have to take all the information you have. I was going to put you to sleep. Do you have any idea of who could be targeting you?"

"There are too many people."

Kizaki exhaled his cigarette smoke quietly.

"But it doesn't seem like I'll be able to take anything from you. I'm just doing this for work. I don't have anything against you. I don't know anything about you. I'll just run away from Yata already. But I don't think you'd send someone home after they came to get you."

I stood up.

"If you'll let me go in exchange for sex, you should have sex with me. Do what you want to my body, as many times as you want. Just don't kill me."

I took off the straps of my dress, and headed toward the bed. I half-hid my body with my falling dress, but exposed my legs and sat on the bed.

"If you'll forgive me, please, hurry and do it. It's too miserable like this."

Kizaki cut across the darkness and came toward me. His body was broad and big. He took off his necktie. I couldn't breathe. He kneeled on the bed, and covered my body with his.

"Before that, take the stun gun off your hip."

I felt a dull pain in my heart. I got off the bed, stuck

my hand through the false bottom of my purse, and grabbed the pistol there. Chest heaving, I pointed the muzzle at Kizaki.

"Oh."

"I'll really shoot. Do what I tell you."

I felt strange holding a gun. On it was carved M3913. It was an American gun made for women. Yata had given me this gun. It really stood out in this room. It overflowed with presence, and confused me. It was so exotic—it looked more like it should belong to Kizaki than to myself. It felt as though I was getting closer to him through this black gun. I was approaching the inexplicable, unhappy world where he belonged. Why was I trying to smile at a moment like this?

"Hurry. I don't have much patience."

"You can't shoot."

I had to shoot. Facing this incomprehensible man, I had no choice but to take that kind of action. I couldn't shoot his leg. I aimed for his stomach. I had shot guns before, when I'd been abroad. If I missed, I might hit his heart, but that was something to think about when that time came. For now, I needed to get out of here. I had to do it to keep living.

"I'll shoot. I'm going to shoot."

"If you're going to do it, do it." Kizaki laughed a little. "When you pull that trigger, you'll understand just what kind of world you're living in."

There was pressure on my chest, and something was crawling up my throat. My whole body was being pulled toward the trigger. I tensed my shoulders and pulled the trigger. There was a dry sound, and my vision shook. There were no bullets.

I noticed it the moment I felt that dull pain in my heart. Behind me, there was a gun pointed at my head.

9.

THE MAN BEHIND me, reflected in the window, was wearing a plain coat. If he had been hiding in this room, where had he been? The skin on my head where that gun was pointed began to go numb. I couldn't feel my legs, but somehow I kept standing.

"Why?" I whispered. Kizaki stood in front of me, laughing slightly.

"The bullets? They're here." Bullets tumbled from Kizaki's hand to the table.

"But when . . ."

"There was time. When you were watching the show."

My body was losing strength.

"Don't tell me you were so engrossed you didn't notice? I had one of my men search you. As for the bracelet, I figured I could find out what was in there later."

"Too dangerous . . ." said the man behind me. "This woman is brave, but she's no pro. If she were . . ."

"You can tell whether she's a pro from looking at her."

The room went cold.

"Well, shall I kill her?"

Kizaki leaned back on the sofa and sipped his drink. "The only problem is the body. Should we wrap it up?"

"Certainly. There are men waiting in the hall. All we need is five minutes to get her out of here."

"You have three. Be quick about it."

"Understood." The man behind me took a quiet breath, as if to prepare himself.

"I love looking at people who know they are about to die," Kizaki said. He was looking at me, his mouth twisted. "I don't kill many people. Personally, that is.

I prefer to watch them die like this. He's killed many, though. How does it feel? How does it feel to kill someone?" Kizaki asked the man behind me.

"The first time I killed someone, I needed a woman after."

"And now?"

"I just need a little alcohol."

Kizaki laughed and took another sip of his drink. He moved his hand like he was signaling something.

"Wait." I tried to gain control of my wild mind, and somehow, I got those words out. I couldn't breathe properly. "But I still don't understand why. I . . ."

"I like watching people who don't know why they're dying."

I looked at him blankly.

"Why did this happen, they think," he said. "How did I get dragged in like this? Why am I going to die? I like watching people die, trapped in that whirlpool of non-sensicalness."

I wondered why I'd come here. It was bound to turn out like this. Why did I try to rush straight into the lair of someone who wanted to drag me down? If I hadn't come, Yata would have killed me. But besides that, I felt the heat inside me, inviting me here. That heat was gone now. It would have been better if that heat kept burning like a fire inside me until the moment I died. But it vanished, as if its role was done. As if to betray me.

"But I'm in a good mood right now," Kizaki said. "I'll tell you a little bit. When I stop talking, you die."

The lights of the buildings outside the window were being turned off one by one.

"Why did you lie to get close to me?" I asked.

Kizaki began tapping his fingers on the table.

"I wasn't lying. I own many businesses and organizations, including many orphanages."

"What?"

"Of course I don't actually go there myself. I'm not the manager of the place. I just give them money. It's a means to take control of those kids' lives. Interesting people come from places like that. People like you . . ."

I stared at Kizaki silently.

"But, before we get to that, let me tell you one thing. Did you know that there are four versions of the Gospel?"

What was he saying? I watched him, the gun still pressed against my head.

"There is this great passage in the Gospels of Mark and Matthew. The words they say Christ screamed when he was nailed to the cross. 'My God, my God, why hast thou forsaken me?' Isn't that great? Don't you think? The son of a carpenter was given powers by God. He used those powers to perform miracles, gain many followers and face the ancient forces of the world. But when he was caught and nailed to the cross, he lost all his powers, like it was timed. Even though the very reason he was arrested was the power he had wielded until then. In that crucial moment, there were no miracles. Don't you think it's great to imagine the hopelessness Christ must have felt when he was betrayed by God?"

Kizaki's smoke climbed silently to the ceiling.

"Of course, after that, Christ rose from the dead, and it's presumed he knew he would come back. But then why did he scream 'why hast thou forsaken me'? It's strange. What if it wasn't true? What if he didn't rise from the dead, and he just died there on that cross? It would become a tragic story. Wouldn't it? Jesus would just be a man made to dance by God, and then betrayed. But Christianity spread thanks to his death. Just as it's written in the Bible. The thing about a single grain of wheat. If it doesn't die, it's just a single grain. But from its death comes many grains. What I really love about this story is that four hundred years before Christ, something similar happened on this earth. The case of Socrates. I'm sure you know his name at least. He was a Greek philosopher."

I had no idea what he was talking about.

"He could hear voices in his head. That qualified him to become a prophet. But he was such a modest man, he refused that title. He worshipped the existing Greek gods too passionately to start a religion of his own. He became an outcast because of his speculative powers, and ultimately, he was taken to court. He could have pleaded to have his sentence reduced, and gotten by without dying, but instead he forcefully asserted his beliefs. The officials frowned on his behavior, so he was sentenced to death. But what's most interesting about this story is the quality of the voices Socrates heard."

The man behind me pressing the gun to my head did not move at all.

"Apparently, those voices never told him what to do. They only stopped him from doing things. Socrates was grateful to those voices. He thought they were sacred. He lived his life obeying those voices. When he wanted to do something, if he didn't hear a voice, he'd do it. If he heard a voice, he'd stop. When he was on trial, he didn't hear any voices. He did not ask for his sentence to be reduced, and even when he expressed his beliefs to the court, the voices did not stop him. He thought his actions followed the will of the gods, so he continued to agitate the judges. But, in the end, he got the death sentence."

Kizaki laughed a little.

"He accepted his death as the will of the gods. He was quite the brave man. And because of his death, his words were passed on to later generations. Don't you think these cases are remarkably similar? Both were guided by gods, betrayed, and because of their cruel deaths, their names lived on. It's safe to assume that this kind of thing occurs all the time in this world.

Don't you think the gods are most happy when they do things like that? That's what I want to do."

"What is?" What was he saying?

"I was carrying out one of my plans. It was going too well, so I wanted to change things up. Then I saw you. Yurika Kajima. You were taken in by the Kashiwagi Orphanage nineteen years ago. Of all the kids, you were the most beautiful girl with the most evil eyes. How perfect. I thought I'd write your story for you. I'd use Hasegawa to call you to the orphanage, and make you grow attached to the children there. At that orphanage, there's this child there whose face looks just like Shota's, the kid you tried to save."

My chest began to hurt. I still didn't understand.

"You would be drawn to that child because of your life experience up until now, and your personal inclinations. You would recall Shota along the way. And then you would begin doing a certain sort of work to save that child. Of course, that is work we planned for you, work that would draw you beautifully, deeply into one part of our plan. You would succeed at that job, and do more work for us. With a little help from us, you'd get through even more dangerous situations. But, in the end, the very end, when you most need help, we'd suddenly forsake you, and you'd die. And if I, the director of the orphanage, showed up then, you wouldn't understand why. You would have died with a great look on your face. And then, I planned on writing your will, right in front of your eyes."

"My will?"

"To further reinforce the story we wrote for you. We planned to *rewrite* your past in that will. There are countless people in history whose lives have been rewritten. No one should ever believe history happened as we pass it down. People's lives are rewritten all the time by those in power and because of the circumstances of history itself. They are made villains and heroes. There's no way to prove that Christ and Socrates's lives were really as we've heard them. You would move through the story we wrote you, and then, after we rewrote your life in your will, you would take responsibility for several crimes you didn't commit, and die cruelly. In the underworld, you'd live on as something of a legend. Yours would be the story of the beautiful prostitute who helped bring about a tremendous change."

"Why me?"

"Hm?"

"Why?"

I looked up at Kizaki. He was dark, big.

"Why you? Do you really think there's a reason for everything that happens in this world? Why did that child die instead of this one? Why did I set my eyes on you instead of that woman? It's because the world has always been that way. The only choices we have to make in this world are unforgiving, offhand ones. Why me? People have been asking that since long ago. The one who enjoys this world the most is God. That is, if God exists. God writhes, feasting on the chains of good and evil that each human life creates unendingly. There's no way that the god of this world, where good people and children die left and right, is as sweet as people think."

He stopped there and took a breath.

"Simply put, this is a game. And I'm bored."

He smiled silently. My body began to go limp. I realized there was a presence before me that I'd never understand. I never thought I'd understood my life, but now, at the end, I was seeing this man. The air went dry.

"But our plans went awry. You didn't go along with our invitation. Even though Hasegawa kept inviting you so persistently."

Kizaki laughed quietly.

"It seems that there was some *error*. That error made for my entertainment. There was a man with a two percent chance of surviving a certain encounter. He made it, and it was such an impressive feat, I just let it pass. *I never thought that he would wind up connected to you like this.* But this has turned out to be pretty fun. Just when I was thinking generally of another way to draw you in, my interests and Yata's came into conflict. That man at the hotel in Ikebukuro. We needed to kill him. That moment was incredibly enjoyable. Because of that moment, you would have to approach me, despite my initial error. I expected Yata would send you to that room with the murdered man. And then, after that, Yata would send you after me."

Kizaki stood up.

"The plans changed, but in the end, I get to see you die a cruel, meaningless death. I'll consider myself fulfilled. Don't worry. We will write your will. As we want it. We'll write it for the sake of our plans, and to have you take on a few of our crimes. You look pale."

He closed in on me, and brought his face up to mine.

"If there were people watching you now, do you know what they'd think?"

My eyes teared up.

"They'd think, *it's her own fault*. You didn't live as a proper citizen. You got involved in the underworld, so it's only natural. The world is cruel. People only judge others angrily."

Kizaki kissed me on the lips. He put his tongue in my mouth, and while persistently licking the back of my tongue, he grabbed my chest. Though I was going to be killed, the heat deep inside my body began to flicker, as if resisting something.

"Now you're at your most beautiful. You might even have turned me on. Kill her."

Kizaki rose from the bed. I could sense the man behind me moving slightly.

"Wait . . ."

Kizaki turned just a bit, and looked down at me.

"Give me a fake."

"Fake what?"

"Give me fake information. I'll give that to Yata."

My body kept losing its strength, but I focused and spoke. Why do I cling to my life, even in these circumstances?

"Yata's your enemy. He's not as weak as you think. If I give him fake information, you can trick him. And then I can steal the information you need from him. All Yata has to control me is money. Instead of killing me, you can still use me."

Kizaki laughed.

"The scream of life. You're screaming out that you can still be useful to this world."

The man behind me backed up, and Kizaki threw a USB drive at me. As if he'd had it prepared the whole time.

"Give that to him. We'll be in touch to tell you what we'll need you to do next."

10.

THE MAN POINTING the gun at me led me out of the room. He followed as I walked down the hall. We cut through the lobby, lit by countless garish chandeliers, and outside there was a car waiting. Were they going out of their way to drop me off?

I sat in the back. Hasegawa was in the driver's seat. He eased his foot onto the gas. I couldn't think properly, so I just looked out the window. The city continued to emanate obscene light. It had no regard for me. The moon was hidden behind the clouds, and I couldn't see it. If it appeared, what would it look like to me?

"I'm sorry," said Hasegawa, his hands gripping the steering wheel. "I'm not sure what to say."

"You're not Hasegawa, are you?"

"What do you mean? Well, I guess I'm not the same person I used to be."

Was he Hasegawa? The question alone depressed me.

"I didn't think it would turn out this way. With you getting dragged in like this . . ."

"Stop lying."

"All right. I guess it doesn't matter what I say."

The lights of the red-light district shined happily. I saw a sign for TOUCHY TOUCHY KINTARO, and smiled in spite of myself. No matter what situation a person's in, they can smile. I saw a sign for MISSION DICK POSSIBLE, and smiled again.

"Nothing ever goes well," Hasegawa said. "No matter what I do."

What was he trying to say all of a sudden? There's really nothing as boring as a man's personal talk.

"I had no place to live, so I started staying at saunas.

I thought if I stayed at an Internet café, it would be filled with people like me and I'd get depressed, but the saunas were no different. I worked day jobs, and used that money for a place to stay and the day's food. I spent the rest on my cell phone bill, and saved a little bit to rent another apartment. It was pretty depressing to spend just a couple hundred yen every day. One day, when I was sitting in the lobby of a sauna, a man came up to me. I saw his new leather shoes stomp across the dirty floor. He was tall and had on an expensive-looking suit. He was Kizaki's subordinate."

I stared out the window. There was even a bar called POWER RANGERS MARRIED WOMEN FORCE.

"That man, out of nowhere, he just threw all this money at me. One million yen. And then he said, 'You've got an interesting look in your eyes,' and he asked, 'Do you want to rise to the top? Will you do some dirty work?' I shook a little. It was like my boring life was suddenly going to change."

We left the red-light district, passed through a shopping area, and entered a residential area where there was nothing but streetlights.

"I did a lot of work. I mostly worked as Kizaki's driver, but I also delivered bags with who knows what inside, and snuck into diplomats' homes. It was like I was being revitalized from the inside out. That man, he makes fiction out of our boring world."

"How childish to be so happy about something like that."

Hasegawa started to say something, but he shut up. I hadn't gotten tangled up with Kizaki because of Hasegawa's invitations, so what happened from here was not his fault. But I wanted to be mean to him. It didn't really have anything to do with logic. It was just to make myself feel better.

"Your life was boring, so you're happy now that you get to play underworld fixer. Getting involved with you would be such a pain in the ass."

"That's not what I planned to do. They said to volunteer at the orphanage. That was where I grew up, and I like kids anyway, so I did it. They said they wanted to ask you to do some simple work, so . . ."

"And you trusted them? You idiot."

"I also thought I'd be able to see you again," Hasegawa

said as he stopped the car at a red light. "It was because I thought I could see you again, Yurika."

He was so stupid. He was just a normal man who happened to have been a big part of my childhood. My cigarette had gone out because I forgot to smoke it, so I lit it again. There was no moon to see anymore.

I GOT OFF in an alley far from the hotel, waited for him to drive away, and began walking. They must have known where the hotel was, so that was all pointless. A man who looked like some sort of businessman walked toward me, staring. He was probably on his way home. In his hand was a convenience store bag with a comic book and a can of beer. When I met his gaze with an unfriendly expression, he casually took his eyes off of me. His appearance made me feel a little better. The next man who walked by me and the man after that both looked at me. I glared back at them, unhappy.

When I returned to my hotel room, the door was open. I had expected this. The room was a mess. They had opened all the drawers, as if to let me know I was being monitored.

I exhaled, sat on the sofa, and lit another cigarette. The pain in my feet upset me. I took off my high heels. They say that the angle of a woman's ankles when she wears high heels is the same as the angle her ankles make when she orgasms. Somehow, I doubt that. They also say high heels originated with ancient Greek prostitutes. That I actually wonder about. But now none of that mattered. For some reason the table was wet. I took off my stockings. I felt like I had come a long way. And when I realized all my life had amounted to was this trashed room, it seemed a little funny. I gripped the knife in my bag and thought about the man who took it from me. I felt like I'd never meet him again. Like Kizaki had said, meeting him was some sort of error, some sort of mistake. This knife might not be enough to get me out of trouble anymore. I took a beer from the refrigerator, but it was too cold so I didn't drink it. Even taking off my makeup was too much work.

I DON'T REMEMBER when I started carrying this knife. It feels like I've had it for as long as I can remember. I used to hide it from everyone around me. I don't think this is what actually happened, but wouldn't it be interesting if my parents who abandoned me, whose faces I've never even seen, gave it to me? They left me. They forsook me. But they gave me a knife. If my parents did that, I'd like to see their faces. But I probably just picked it up. I have a faint memory of reaching through the gaps in a fence by some park and grabbing it with my fingers.

When I was in elementary school, my classmates bullied me. Their bullying just kept escalating. If they had just taken my things and hidden them, that would have been fine, but the girls would get together and beat me up. They wouldn't have been brave enough if they hadn't been in a group. I rolled this knife up in my gym clothes and carried it with me. Then, one day, I found myself surrounded by the laughter of girls whose faces I can't recall. They pushed me over. They surrounded me, forming a circle. The circle began shrinking. When they closed in on me and toppled me to the ground, I reached into the bag with my gym clothes, grabbed this knife, and stood up. I faced them and waved it around.

I remember clearly the line I drew with this knife. I didn't hit any of the girls, but this knife cut cleanly through the air in front of their startled faces. They never expected to see a naked weapon there like that. It was too strange for such a place. That knife drew a straight, black line. It was a world apart from the dull unsightliness of those girls, and the sand on the exercise field, and my pitifulness, and my old backpack. Its overwhelming presence stuck out sharply. That blackness was too beautiful, too straight. The girls went silent. I fell for the beauty of that powerful line. I imagined it continuing on, slicing through the obstacles in my life one after another. I looked at that line jealously. I wanted to see it again. When I fixed my grip on the knife with my small hand, the girls around me backed away.

And then they stopped bullying me. No one ever became my friend, but I didn't mind. I knew that line would distance me from the good people as well, but I didn't mind.

I WOKE UP lying on the sofa. My makeup had caked up with my sweat and felt disgusting, so I took my makeup remover to the bathroom. The rings around my eyes were particularly dark. I was tired. I couldn't hear any of the city's night sounds in this hotel room. I was tired and alone. I remembered a black cat I had seen long ago between two buildings. It was pregnant, lying on its side. That cat had carried its big belly there, and alone in the vast darkness of the night endured the mysterious fear of having unknown life wiggling inside it, trying to get out. I lit a cigarette and lay down on the bed. I was confused. I had to get some real sleep.

My phone rang. I couldn't breathe. I stared at the phone as if it were trying to corner me. Though it was my own possession, it seemed like it should belong to some terribly disgusting person I didn't know. The number was blocked, but I answered. It was a man. His voice was low. He said he worked for Kizaki.

"We want a list of all the men you've tricked. And all of the photos and videos you've taken."

"I've given all of that to Yata. I don't have it. I can't give it to you."

"We also want copies of all of Yata's negotiations."

"I can't get that. It must all be on Yata's personal

computer or his hard drives. I don't even know where it is. And I don't know his passwords."

He hung up. I listened closely as my heart began to race, the phone still in my hand.

At some point, I saw the moon. It was covered by thin clouds, but behind them it was overflowing with light. Just like the night Eri died.

11.

I TOOK THE west exit of Ikebukuro station and walked through a crowd of people. There were Christians shouting through a microphone about how the end was coming, and a drugstore employee repeating the names of makeup products that were on sale. A man carrying a guitar was setting up an amplifier, and hosts called out to gaudily dressed girls. There were noisy, drunk men and women, touts, and women in exposing clothes. This is the bustle of the night, filled with desire.

The natural, raw chaos, set free from the afternoon. As I moved through the crowd, I pulled out my phone. Drunk retirees were crouching on the sidewalk.

"I'm going to walk toward you. Follow me."

"All right."

I passed one stoplight, and took the road across from the Marui department store. Kimura, the tout, was there. He stuck both of his hands in his pockets and leaned in toward me.

"I need a fake passport," I said.

Kimura's long brown hair gently reflected the neon lights.

"All right. I'll pass that on."

"When will it be finished?"

"For a good one, it will take at least six days."

He walked along next to me.

"Do it in five, please. Am I being followed?"

"No, I don't think so. There are two weird-looking guys, but it's probably nothing."

"Two?"

"You usually use three people to tail someone."

We walked to the corner in front of a business hotel.

Touts are in charge of a limited area, so he couldn't go any further than that. I put an envelope with my picture in the pocket of his trench coat. I felt his body heat slightly with my fingers.

"Use these pictures. Text me how much it'll cost."

Kimura looked at my chest and neck.

"You don't have to pay my part of the fee in money."

"You idiot," I said, and turned at the corner. He laughed and turned around. Men who aren't desperate for women shouldn't be so insistent. I turned down a dimly lit road. It was wet for some reason. There were neon signs for hostess bars and topless joints. There was a tout whose face I couldn't quite make out standing, looking cold. When I turned around, I didn't see anyone following me. Was it just my nerves? I walked down the even darker street, where the foreign Asian women stood, and there, at the end of it, was Yata's car. I repeated in my head the things I would do to him. I had secretly saved the pictures of the men I tricked, so I could give those to Kizaki. The problem was getting my hands on all of the documents Yata had, what Kizaki's man called his "negotiations." I had no time to think about why he had those things, or what he was. I approached his car. My heart was pounding so hard it hurt.

Suddenly, my phone rang. I stared at Yata's car as I answered the phone slowly. It was from Yata, in the car.

"Did you take the bullets from the gun?"

"Yeah."

"Leave them in the bag. Hand them to the man in the suit. He's coming now."

A man trotted toward me. He took the paper bag from me, and without making a real effort to hide what he was doing, confirmed the contents casually. He walked away. The back door was open, but I went for the passenger door. Yata scrunched his eyebrows a bit, but he opened the door for me.

"What?"

"It seems like I've been spotted by someone. I'm nervous. Let's go somewhere else."

Yata stepped on the gas quietly. The car sewed through alleyways, taking us even deeper into the darkness.

"You wouldn't just give me a gun for self-defense," I said, watching the road. "You were hoping that if things went well, I'd kill that man when I got cornered. Weren't you? If I did, I'd have nowhere to run, and I would die too . . . You would erase our secret relationship without hiring anyone else. That would have cleaned up this situation very economically, and even more important, secretly. Am I wrong?"

Yata's expression did not change when I asked.

"Even if I told you to kill him, you wouldn't have listened to me. But I did think you might kill him if you had a gun. I didn't hope for it, though. I just thought that if you did kill him, that would be convenient. And I didn't plan it. You're the one who asked for a gun."

"Well, it doesn't matter anymore."

The smell of my perfume spread through the car. I quietly crossed my legs, bare below my short skirt, to keep up a natural appearance. I wondered if it would work. The car finally pulled into a silent parking lot. I handed Yata the USB drive.

"Really? So it went well?"

I replied to Yata's question with a stern face. Depressed-looking Asian women walked in and out of the many buildings standing in the darkness. I heaved a drawn-out sigh.

"He seemed to like me. He kept fucking me. Over and over."

Yata didn't look at me, but I stuck out my chest in case he looked my way.

"He knew I was sent by you."

"Really?"

"He knew a lot about you. He thought I was your woman. It seemed like he was getting off on stealing your woman and seeing what she was like. When he was fucking me, he kept asking who was better, you or him. And then I had to say, over and over, that he was better."

Yata kept staring straight ahead.

"Anyway, how did you steal this?"

"I think his weakness is women. He told me to leave you, and I pretended to agree. I had to. If I didn't, I wouldn't have been able to get out of there. I waited for him to fall asleep, and got into his computer. I couldn't get into the blocked part, so this might not be what you want."

I took a breath.

"I'm good at making men think that I'm theirs and theirs alone. I believe I've done exactly what you asked. But these files might be a decoy. So don't blame me if the information is inaccurate. Be sure to check whether it's real or not. If this doesn't satisfy you, and if you won't let me go after this, I've got no choice, so I'll go back."

I thought about the passport I had asked Kimura for. The passport I needed to get away.

"I see."

"And . . ." I had to maintain a calm face so he couldn't tell my pulse was speeding up. My breathing was starting to go wild too, but I got it under control. "He said to leave you. Become his woman. He asked me to steal all kinds of information from you. He said he needed to see your negotiations."

My heart was racing. I felt an intense heat deep inside my body. This was the only way to save myself.

"So give me a fake. If you do, I can trick him."

12.

WOMEN WRAPPED ONLY in thin cloth were drunk in the town square.

Floralia. The festival of prostitutes in Ancient Rome. The exuberant, raw ecstasy the people had before the birth of the strict religion Christianity. During Floralia, they also held *orgia*, secret ceremonies, orgies conducted and controlled by noblewomen. The line between nobility and prostitutes vanished, and women set free their sexuality. The transparent light of the full moon illuminated the women.

Women got drunk, danced, and laughed. They dragged in men, and made them their slaves. Women's wails and laughter rose, spiraling into the air. I felt like I was both amongst those women and slightly removed, like a tree in the distance watching them. The moon's great gravity made wild the distant seas. The women clamored, wet with sweat. One of the women reached out a pale hand to offer me alcohol. I had only seen her in pictures, but I think she was actually the prostitute Phryne. Those too-big almond eyes and thick lips had to have been hers. They were too beautiful. She pointed to a trench. In it were people wearing animal skins. They were removed from the world, praying to the moon to forget themselves completely and transcend all. They lit fires, rubbed opium into their skin, and chanted prayers that had been passed down since ancient times.

Make me one who eats men
Make me one who eats women
Make me one who eats children

Give me blood
Give me human blood
Give it to me tonight
My heart, my body, my soul, I give them all to you

Phryne took off her robe and showed her supple chest. She kissed me gently. My body grew hot. She said I was beautiful, and for some reason I teared up. The wails around me grew louder, and someone removed my clothes. Madwomen were chosen as the priestesses of this festival. There was Elizabeth Báthory of Hungary, who killed hundreds of young women to restore her own youth. There was Queen Nzinga of Angola, who crushed six hundred people for their blood, who made men fight to the death and took the winner as her personal sex slave. They stared up at the moon, mixed with the wild women, and drank human blood. The enormous moon came closer. It was approaching the pure ecstasy of those women, the ecstasy that surpassed good and evil. Those drunk women shouted. They beckoned the moon, and it came closer.

—*Inside you*

Someone spoke that to me while I stared up at the moon. But I also heard it come from inside myself. The moon was closing in. Deep within that light, I could clearly see its rough surface. It approached gradually, casually, as if to show that it was the heavenly body that controlled the earth. It was too large. The women laughed. They continued to scream screams of joy.

—*Inside you*

The moon's gravity was too strong. It dragged away my consciousness. The woman I thought was Phryne wrapped her arms around me softly. The people in the pit standing around a fire continued to pray to the moon.

My heart, my body, my soul. I give it all to you

The ceiling light struck my eyes. My chest felt heavy, and I was sweating. *Inside you.* The voice lingered within me. The voice from my dream wouldn't let me calm down. What was inside me? Resignation? Causeless obstinacy?

I was in a different hotel room than yesterday. When I opened the curtain, I could see the moon beyond the buildings outside. It shone brightly, and was getting close to full. Native Americans passed down this quaint legend. They said that the moon used to be as bright as the sun, but it gave up part of its light to let people sleep. I don't know about that, though. I want to change it. I want to say instead that the moon gave up part of its light so people could let loose their desires in the darkness. The moon kept only the evil light, the light that illuminates those hidden desires.

WHEN I WENT to the café on the first floor, Hasegawa was already there. The down jacket hanging on his seat looked fake. When I approached him, he gave me a weak smile. It was a pretentious café where serious people gather. The coffee was expensive, but so tasteless you couldn't drink it without sugar.

"For a start . . ."

I handed him a USB and copies of documents. There were a few pictures that I had saved secretly, and the forged documents that Yata had given me. If they worked off of these documents, they'd get into trouble. It was information about overseas insider trading and powerful oil-traders who were coming to Japan. The insider trading information was fake, but the information about the oil-traders was real. Their deal was quite valuable, but it was illegal. Their behind-the-scenes trades were already being monitored by the justice department, so if someone tried to get involved they'd get found out. I felt a slight heat in my body. I made a tired face and watched Hasegawa put that all away in his bag.

"Wasn't it dangerous? To get this?" Hasegawa asked in a small voice. We had only been together for a few minutes, but he had already looked at my chest three times.

"That has nothing to do with you."

"Yeah. You're right."

I deliberately sipped my tasteless coffee.

"But if they make you do something else . . . It'll just get worse."

Suddenly, I felt a fluttering inside me. I had this silly feeling that even though I wanted nothing to do with him, I had to be nice to him.

"It has nothing to do with you. Don't make me say it again."

"I have this dream," he said out of nowhere.

What was he talking about? He really was an idiot.

"I'll save money. And then I'll start a foundation for all the children sick of the world." He looked at me with clear eyes. "Until children are full-grown, they can't handle life on their own. I want to help them. And then, I'll choose some of the orphans to raise. I want to bring up children who will shock the world."

There was a string instrument solo playing on the café's speakers.

"I saw myself doing it all in Japan. But I could do it overseas too. Actually, when I think about it, it might be better to do it overseas. So . . ."

He looked at me again.

"If they demand you do something this dangerous again, will you run away with me?"

My hand holding the cigarette froze. I could tell from his face and voice that he was speaking from the bottom of his heart. But why? It made me uncomfortable.

"Won't you get killed?"

"It's fine. I have a plan."

My discomfort grew. Why? I forced myself to finish my tasteless coffee, and he picked up his phone.

"Wait a second. I have to let them know."

He called, but because there were a lot of connections, it took a long time to get to Kizaki. When he finally started speaking, he kept his voice down, so I couldn't hear him well. The music in the restaurant seemed loud. He handed me his cell phone.

Now I had to focus on my conversation with Kizaki. I gave Hasegawa one last good look, since I would have to shift my attention away from him. He was looking at my body. His eyes were tinged with passion, and I could also sense a slightly mad darkness there. Every man's desires are slightly mad, but his, for some reason, made me uncomfortable. I wondered why. But I had no time to think. Kizaki was speaking.

"Tell me about the situation."

I noticed my pulse gradually speeding up, but I took a quiet breath so he wouldn't notice.

"I didn't take it directly from Yata. I asked one of the men close to him."

I felt a slight heat in my body. This kind of story needed to sound as realistic as possible.

"That subordinate did everything I asked. He was already unhappy with Yata, and he's stupid. He was also obsessed with me. If you want, I can even introduce him to you. He's pretty close to Yata."

Kizaki was silent. I took another deep breath, hoping they didn't notice anything.

"But I don't know if Yata has checked that information yet. It might be raw. So don't blame me if the information is inaccurate."

The heat continued to burn inside me.

"Yata gathers a lot of information. So check it. If that doesn't satisfy you, I'll try again. But this time, give me a job I can actually pull off."

My body was tense. My fingers were probably trembling. I stopped my hand as I reached for my cigarette.

"Good answer," Kizaki replied quietly. My heart was racing. "First we have to check it. I'll have my subordinates do it. Tell Hasegawa to come back right away."

He hung up. My body gradually relaxed. If it was dangerous to be on either side, I wouldn't join either. I'd be in over my head, but since I was already this deep, it was the only way to save myself. Fool both sides, evade responsibility to buy time, and gracefully slip between the two. To put them off guard I had to make it look like I was working for them until the moment before I ran away. I thought about the fake passport I had asked Kimura for. Four more days.

13.

"IT'S REAL."

I could tell it was Yata's voice, but for some reason, maybe because I had just woken up, he sounded terribly far away.

"We more or less understand him now. Not completely, but that was pretty valuable information. For someone with such a reputation, his defenses are pretty weak."

I fixed my hold on the phone. What was he talking

about? Kizaki had handed that information over to me intentionally. I didn't understand.

"Really? Well then, am I done? He really tires me out. He's too much."

"Too much what?"

I felt something in his voice. Not quite jealously, but maybe something similar. I didn't know if it would work, but to dull his judgment, I said, "You don't understand? He's too . . . talented."

"The money's at the front desk."

He hung up. The room's cold fluorescent lights felt incredibly intense. Yata was not the kind of man to make a mistake about the accuracy of information. Why had Kizaki given me real information? I didn't know. My chest fluttered slightly, but I was already done with all that. Three more days.

I thought further about how things had gotten to this point. It had started when I took the job from Yata. But if I traced it back further, it had really started with Shota. I'd needed a lot of money right away. I'd wanted something I couldn't get with my own skills, and I'd wanted it fast, so I stepped into this unnatural world and wound up working with Yata. But I didn't regret it.

I had made all those choices myself. I may have done things the wrong way, but I don't care about common sense or what other people think. Given the situation I had gotten myself into, I just chose the path that seemed most likely to succeed and did the best I could.

But Shota died so suddenly. His death ripped open a deep fissure in my life. It was a cruel and heedless truth that I will never be able to comprehend. No matter what I do, I cannot change it. Is there any meaning in this world where Shota could die such an inexplicable death? That fissure spread through me unexpectedly. A responsible person would probably tell me to smile even though he's gone. They'd probably say Shota, even though he was only a child, would have wanted me to lead a good life. But I don't need to hear those words. This world is overflowing with hackneyed expressions like that. They can comfort most people, but they make me suffer. Words that most people nod along to make those who can't nod along suffer. They alienate them. What about words that can reach someone like me? Do those exist? I am twisted. I can't look at the world straight. But why am still trying to live on? Even though I think it would be better to curse the world, smile perversely and die.

I got a message from Kimura. He gave me the information for the account I needed to transfer the money to, and said that the passport would be ready on December sixth, according to plan. I sent him a thank-you message, made some black tea, and drank just a little of it. After I get the passport, all that was left was to get to the airport without being noticed. Just in case either side was watching me, I couldn't make any suspicious moves. White light refracted painfully in my tea.

I got the envelope Yata sent from the front desk and left the hotel. It wouldn't seem strange for me to deposit this money. I went to an ATM, and after depositing it in my account, I transferred money to the account Kimura instructed. There were no other people in this cold, mechanical space. Even if someone was watching me from afar, they couldn't see exactly what I was doing.

As I walked through the lights of the city at night, I felt colder and colder. I'm used to being alone, but

I thought my current situation was special. Kizaki had said there was a kid who looked like Shota at the orphanage. I wanted to see him, but that would definitely be dangerous. If they created a weakness within me, I wouldn't be able to run away, and that kid's life would also be endangered. I went into a bar, sat at the counter, and ordered a whiskey and hot water. I couldn't think logically. I was tired. The man at the end of the bar was looking at me. His hair was short, he was clean-cut, his shoulders were wide, and his suit looked good on him. He didn't look tied down, and his eyes had a certain strength to them. Should I get drunk and sleep with him now? But I could see that I would regret that so much I would want to die after. I didn't want to get involved with anyone, and I didn't want to bear being alone with the warmth left by someone long gone.

Suddenly, my phone rang. I couldn't breathe. The number was blocked. It was Yata. Was I found out? It was too soon for him to be calling again. Something was wrong. But I'd told him from the start that I wouldn't take responsibility for that information.

"Tomorrow, nine P.M. Go to room 606 in Hotel La Perte. It's by the north exit of Ikebukuro."

I lit a cigarette to get my shaking under control.

"Why?"

"Take pictures and film the man there. He's a man who surfaced from the information you stole. We need to create a weakness for him."

I had a bad feeling. Kizaki had probably given me that information knowing this would happen. But why? What was in it for him? My chest made an awful noise.

"Hasn't the turnaround been fast lately? Why me again?"

Yata was silent. I can't do anything suspicious, I thought. I took a quiet breath.

"I want money too. But I'm going to wear myself out. If you could give me a little more time between jobs, I'd really appreciate it."

"I'll think about it. Do this job and send me the pictures. I can't get close this time. If something happens, call the number I'm going to give you. My subordinate will answer."

"Got it."

Yata told me the number and hung up. I thought I had gotten a little closer to Yata and his people. The man at the edge of the bar was still looking at me. If I drank any more, I didn't know what I'd end up doing. I left without looking at him. The city's neon kept shining. The moon was near full. Even when the moon shrinks and disappears, it shows itself again gradually. When ancient people saw that eternal cycle of death and recovery, they prayed to the moon for their own rebirth. Rebirth. Will I be reborn? I relaxed slightly and smiled. If I were reborn, what would I become?

It seemed like the dark part where the moon was not quite full would suck something up from the earth. The night was long. How should I spend it by myself?

14.

TWO MORE DAYS.

I walked right past the front desk and waited for the elevator. Hotel La Perte was an old, dirty love hotel. When the light for the sixth floor lit up, I felt the presence of the man I would face. The people at the front desk probably thought I was a prostitute, walking into a hotel like this. I remembered that I was something of the sort, and laughed a little.

My heart had been racing for a long time. I couldn't

shake this bad feeling, but I had no choice but to do my job. The elevator door opened before me—a square, mechanical space, indifferent to me. It had nothing to do with the situation I was about to find myself in. It just carried me up to my fate.

I got off the elevator, and walked past several silent doors. I knocked on the door to room 606, but there was no response. I took a breath, opened the door, and there was Yata. What was happening? I tried to run, but someone pushed me down from behind. It was the man who had checked the gun and walked away with it when I gave it back. Did this mean they found out what I did? But I'd told them from the start, I couldn't be responsible for the quality of that information. It was hard to breathe. Yata sat on the sofa and stared at me emotionlessly.

It was a cheap room. The walls were pink and there was an enormous bed. The lights were also pink, and they hurt my eyes. My body was shaking, but somehow my mind remained calm. I felt a second me ignoring the flustered, surprised one. She was focused on trying to think of a way to escape. The colors I saw were getting too bright. The round glow of the bed light stood out from its surroundings, and the hands of the clock were beautiful and sharp enough to take my breath away. I could feel the slight movement of the air on my cheeks and eyelids. Yata wearily lit a cigarette. He was smoking the same thin menthols that girls smoke. The man behind me pushed me again. I was disgusted by the ease with which he could hold me down.

"What is this?" I asked. My voice didn't falter. "Tell me. I won't understand what's going on if you don't talk."

"That information you gave us was real," Yata said quietly.

He looked tired, but he was calm as always. He was a few meters away, and our eyes were locked.

"The fact that it wasn't perfect also lent to its credibility. But I'm not dumb enough to buy it. Some companies are involved with a governmental organization's secret multi-trillion yen project, and there are multinational corporations working illegally behind the scenes, too . . . That man was trying to use this information to pull off something else. Naturally, we had to check the accuracy of this information. I had one of my subordinates deal with it. He met with several people who handle information in secret, paid several people, scrutinized every detail. It was real. There's no mistake. But he's smart. When we went to verify—which was an unavoidable step—there was a trap."

I checked the position of the man behind me. Even if I surprised him, it didn't seem like I could run away.

"We'd provided some information in return for the illegal work, and that information was picked up by Kizaki. It's hard to believe how far this man's influence extends. If the information he picked up were to be exposed, we'd be in a pretty bad position."

Yata leaned back slowly on the sofa.

"It was clear from that skillfully planted trap that this information had been passed to us intentionally. There are three possible scenarios. The first is that, as you said, you really stole this information from him. But that's hard to believe. That would mean he let you steal it on purpose. There are too many unpredictable elements involved for that to be likely. You could have gotten scared and come back without anything. The second scenario is that you aren't on either side, and you tricked us both. And you're taking that slippery road to try and escape. It's a dangerous choice, but if you're thinking about self-preservation, it does seem the most effective." My heart made an awful noise.

"Then, the third possible scenario is that you betrayed me, and you're on his side now. The main reason I think this may be true is that you went out of your way to tell me to *check that information*. A few days ago, when you met Hasegawa at that bar, the man he introduced you to, who said his name was Kondo, is certainly this man. Based on that, the third scenario seems the most likely. You asked me for false information to ease my nerves. You betrayed me, and are working with him now."

While Yata's guess was a little bit off, he was basically right. I tried to think. The man behind me was in the way, and there was nothing I could do about it.

"Which is it? The second or the third? I'm asking you."

I felt that if I said it was the second, I'd be killed right there. Yata wouldn't just let me run away, and knowing as much as I did, I doubt Yata would let me live any longer. And I was just one woman with no friends, no one to save me. Someone would find my corpse somewhere, and that would be the end of it. But Yata already thought I had betrayed him. Several misunderstandings led him to that conclusion on his own. That might actually be better for me as well. It would make him angry, but to have me, one of Kizaki's subordinates, under his control would be valuable to him. To protect my life, I need to raise the value of my existence. And I need to tell a few lies. I wondered if it would work.

"You can't answer? Then you'll die."

"Well, in that case, it's the third."

I sat on the ground, staring at the floor. Yata couldn't see, but I was clenching my jaw. I hoped my posture would make him feel I was being defiant even though I had been caught.

"You betrayed me for him. You're an idiot. But it's fine. Tell me everything you know about him."

"If I refuse?"

"You die."

"Hey, is that really you, Yata? Is something wrong?" I spoke quietly, but with anger in my voice.

"What?"

"You're such an idiot. I'm so tired of this." I made my voice a bit hoarse. "Everything is part of his plan. His goal is to make you lose your position, to erase you from this world. You must know that much. First, he had you verify that information. Then, he got the information he needed to trap you. And then what happens? You kill me because you're angry I gave you that information? He planned this all out. Did you check around you when you came into this hotel? What about all of your subordinates? We've been recorded this whole time. He wants to make you into a murderer. Do you think you have complete control of all the police and detectives? You must know that even prosecutors belong to different factions and have their own interests. He's already working with some of them. He even made me write a will. It says that I'm being used by you, and I think you'll kill me eventually. Everything's going just as he planned. You didn't know? The moment you kill me, he'll have evidence, concrete proof from observing you that you committed murder. When he wants to knock people down, he uses the power of the legal system. Hasn't this kind of thing been going on for ages?"

As I spoke I began to think that what I was saying might actually be true. I hadn't written a will, but Kizaki had said he would write one, that he'd rewrite my life. It was probably already planned out carefully. The story of the prostitute working behind the scenes of a certain incident. That's what he had said. Though it hadn't worked out because I hadn't gone to the orphanage, he probably already had another plan. He'd already figured it out. He'd make me take responsibility for a bunch of crimes, and die here like this. My back and neck were freezing, but I was sweating nonetheless.

"Do you understand? *My life itself is a trap.* There's only one thing you can do. Continue to pretend to be fooled by me, and fool him instead. That's your only option. Why can't you understand that?"

Yata stared into my eyes.

"Well then, why do you keep letting yourself be used instead of running away? Even though you know you'll be killed?"

"I thought you knew everything already. I didn't think you'd be fooled by him. I thought you were just pretending to be tricked. I didn't think you'd try to kill me like this."

"But the limit will come one day. What do you plan to do then?"

"I planned to hang around until one of you vanished. Then I'd stick with the winning side. I'm talented. I thought you'd regret killing me. Running away is my very last option. I wouldn't do something that obvious."

The room went quiet. For some reason I felt like I could see the threads of the fabric on the sofa Yata was sitting on.

"I see. It makes sense. But something bothers me," Yata said quietly.

"I give up. Kill me then. Kill me in this hotel that they're watching. It'll be the end of both of us. If you're going to kill me, just do it. I'm tired of this. It's so stupid."

"But I can't let you go."

"So what will you do? You're still not sure?"

At that moment, a phone rang. I couldn't breathe. If

this was Kizaki calling me, I might be in a bad position. But it was Yata's phone. When he answered the phone, his expression changed. He looked like he had when I'd showed him the email assignment someone else had sent me from his account.

"Give him some space, but watch him for a bit."

Yata walked past me, and left the room. The man was left alone with me. He kept his gun pointed at me, but turned on the TV as if he had something on his mind. The news was on. The prime minister of Japan had been attacked by terrorists on a trip to a meeting in an oil-producing country in Africa. He'd died, along with his secretary and bodyguards. Moments later, several diplomats from the implicated ministry had killed themselves. Next there was a report that the corpse of a missing trading company employee had been found, and another that a microbus carrying government agency employees had gotten into an accident. Everyone besides the driver had died. The man behind me said something quietly. When I tried to get up, he pointed the gun at me again. I looked at him straight. He was large.

"Hey, let me go."

"Don't move. And don't talk."

He kept the gun pointed at me. He was wearing a plain, inconspicuous suit. The curtains shook painfully in the breeze of the air-conditioning.

"There's no point. You can't shoot me. Didn't you hear what I just said? If you kill me, Yata won't let that slide. So . . ."

I stood up and sat on the bed.

"Look. No matter what I do, you can't shoot me."

He glared at me. I widened my eyes, willing my cheeks to flush.

"You're alone in a room with a woman, but you're not going to do anything?"

"What?"

"We've got time to kill. I imagined you'd at least try to touch me, all full of desire, and I'd say, 'No,' or 'Don't.'"

I smiled. I was sure he couldn't shoot me, but there was always the chance my plan could backfire. This man must have been scared of getting burned, too. If I could use that fear, I could get him to put his gun down at least once.

"I won't fall for that."

"Fall for what? Ha ha ha. Sounds like you watch too much TV," I said. "You should just kiss me. Touch me as much as you want. No one will ever find out."

"Be quiet."

"You're so boring. Even when I tease you, you still make that same face. You know, I'm probably better than any of the women you've ever had before."

"I won't be provoked."

"Well then, there's no choice."

I ripped open the front of my blouse. The buttons went flying and landed around my feet.

"What are you doing?"

"I'm tearing my clothes. I'm going to say you attacked me."

"What the hell?"

"Yata will be really pissed. You must know that I'm one of his favorites these days. And you couldn't even manage to keep a woman under control. That's a failure in a subordinate. He'll definitely get rid of you."

"Stop it."

"I won't stop. Why should I care what happens to

a man who won't even touch me? I'll take you down with me."

I popped more buttons, and ripped open the hook on my skirt. He clicked his tongue, put the gun down on the sofa, and reached out to try to stop me. As soon as he was almost on top of me, I took the stun gun from my belt and pressed it to his stomach. White cracks of light shot out and a sharp boom ripped through the air. He collapsed, but it wasn't enough to make me feel safe, so I hit him with the stun gun again. He gasped and let out a shriek.

"It would have been nice if you went unconscious like on TV, too."

I held down his chin, turned my ring to face the fake stone down, released the lid and dumped the powder in his mouth.

"It hurts too much to swallow? You do look like you're in pain. But it's fine. I'll help you."

I took a beer out of the fridge, forced open his mouth and poured it in. My body started to get hot. The man looked pained, and like he was going to spit up the beer. I poured in more.

"Don't worry. It's not poison."

15.

ONE DAY LEFT.

I was lying in bed, couldn't even make myself turn on the lights.

The room was quiet and simple, and I could hear a motor crying in the distance. I curled up like a baby. I took a long breath and exhaled. It seemed strange that I was still alive.

It was dark, but on the table in front of me I could see the black gun. I stole it from that man last night. If there had been any other lackeys around, I would have shot them. But Yata's jobs for me were always top-secret, and I hadn't expected him to have too many other men around. Nevertheless, I needed to be careful just in case. I wasn't sure if I could use the gun properly, but I'd have shot even Yata if I had to.

After I'd dealt with that first guy, I'd cracked opened the door and looked down the hall. I took the fire escape instead of the elevator. The air was very cold, and I stopped walking whenever I heard even a small sound. I kept looking over my shoulder. But there was no sign of any more of his men. I changed taxis. I kept changing taxis until I made it to this business hotel in Yokohama.

For some reason I stared at the red and green lights on the heater. I was originally planning to get that passport from Kimura tonight, then go to Narita first thing in the morning. But I didn't have time. I had to leave Japan today, as soon as I got it. I would be using another name, so even if they could somehow see who was going to board what plane, they'd have no way to find me. Once I was abroad, they wouldn't be able to follow me.

I didn't think they'd go through the trouble of following me overseas.

My phone rang. I couldn't breathe. But it was Kimura, so I answered immediately. I never thought I'd have to rely on him like this. But I had no time, so I had no other choice.

"It's ready. Pick it up at eight."

"What should I do?"

"About that . . . I'm being watched."

My heart made an awful noise.

"By who?"

"The police."

I searched for my cigarettes to calm myself down.

"Don't worry. I was just introducing someone to a drug dealer, and I got into some trouble. But I'm being watched, so I can't go anywhere."

I sighed, a sigh that came from uncomfortably deep in my chest.

"So what should I do?"

"Right. So you'll have to get it yourself. Come to the underground parking lot at the Greer Hotel in Ikebukuro at eight. The guy who made it can't show his face either. There will be a black sedan with a Hiroshima license plate. The doors will be unlocked. It'll be in the glove compartment. But don't do anything strange. He'll be nearby."

"And if it's not there?"

"That won't happen. Trust matters a lot in this business, strange as that sounds."

I hung up. Ikebukuro. I didn't want to go. What would I do if the police were there to catch Kimura? That would just be another problem for me. I felt surrounded. Outside my window, the swarm of cruel buildings was semi-hidden by the fog. If I had to worry about the police, it was probably better not to take the gun.

I dyed my hair black, put on glasses, and took with me a big medical mask, the kind people wear out in public when they're scared of catching or spreading the flu. I took the bullets out of the gun, wiped off my fingerprints, and put the gun and bullets in a paper bag. I left the hotel, went into a nearby department store, and in the changing room, changed into casual, nondescript clothes—jeans, a black sweater, and a gray coat. Just to be safe, I bought a new bag and shoes, too. But what should I do with the clothes I'd taken off? I didn't have anyone to send them to. I didn't want to throw them away. All of a sudden, I was sad. My Balenciaga coat and blouse. My Chloé skirt. And my Coach bag and high heels. I liked them. What was I thinking at a time like this?

I looked at the employee who helped me to the changing room. She was too young and beautiful to work at a plain shop like this. She was about the same height as me. Her eyes were red and looked moist. Maybe she was tired.

"Um, these clothes . . ."

"Yes. If you're going to carry them . . ."

"Oh, no. It's just, if you would like them . . ."

She looked at me strangely.

"It's just, I don't need these anymore. I'm going for a more relaxed look now. I'm leaving the country, and I like to give away clothes anyway. They'd look good on you. Take them. Please."

She was confused. Of course she was confused. This was a strange request. But I grew obstinate.

"Please. I'm going to get rid of them anyway, so I'd rather have someone like you take them. Please."

She probably just didn't want to hurt my feelings, but she accepted my offer. That was good. She'd probably wear them. If not, maybe she'd give them to someone who'd look good in them. I left the department store and flagged a cab. I still had to throw away the gun.

We took a long, wide road from Yokohama to Tokyo. I could see the moon above Tokyo. For some reason, it looked like it was beckoning me. Maybe it was because I hadn't slept, but my head felt empty. I leaned into the seat of the car.

"There aren't any cars following us, are there?"

Why was I asking a question like that? I was tired. My body felt heavy.

"None now. Is there something wrong?"

"Nothing. Sorry to ask that. I can just get off here."

"No, no. It's fine. If I see any strange cars, I'll lose them."

I could see the side of the driver's face from the back. He was probably about sixty. For some reason, he was smiling.

"How long have you been a cab driver?"

"I've been doing this for thirty years. You'll be fine. I know a lot of roads."

As I wondered what kind of man this driver was, my phone rang. It was from Hasegawa. I wasn't sure whether I should answer, but I decided they'd think it was suspicious if I didn't. For some reason, he was breathing heavily.

"Oh good. Where are you?"

"Why? What happened?"

There was a lot of noise on the other side of the phone. It was a strange sound. It seemed like it already had me surrounded, but I couldn't make out its shape. The cab window was wet with condensation.

"Kizaki is . . . He's thinking about what job to give you next. But it's dangerous. Really dangerous. So . . ."

I could tell he was taking a deep breath.

"Run away with me."

"You really . . ."

"I'll tell you the details later. Where are you? I've got everything arranged."

"And?"

"I love you. Can't you tell?"

I looked outside the window. Neon I'd never seen in a part of the city I'd never seen. Countless white lights were reflected in the window. He was so cheerful when we were children. Even now, you could see that cheerfulness in his face. I leaned back, gripping my phone.

I don't know how this goes with other people, but usually, when I'm confused about whether or not I should like someone, I already like them. All these feelings of loneliness make me want to go for whatever opportunities present themselves. I want to have sex too, but what I really want is just for someone to hold me tight. But even that could be dangerous. I'm still lonely though, so when someone makes strong advances on me like this, when someone gives me a reason, I usually go along with them.

But I was too tired. I was tired of the pain and pleasure of losing myself in someone else, thinking that I could change my partner, and I was tired of the guilt of taking on a partner I didn't actually like that much. But . . . I thought about this all, and then laughed. This was not the time.

"Stop it. I'm not going anywhere with you."

"Why?"

We passed through one part of the city I didn't know, and entered another.

"I wondered this whole time whether or not you were Hasegawa. It was all so strange. How I met you so randomly. And how even though we were childhood friends, you worked for him."

I couldn't pull my back from the seat.

"You definitely have Hasegawa's face. I didn't really like him, and I don't remember him that well, but you have the same presence, too. But I still can't shake this weird feeling. I'm still not sure if you're Hasegawa. But I know this much. You don't really love me. I've been through a lot, so I can tell that much. Even though you don't love me, you say you do, and you even say we should run away together. That means you're, at the very least, my enemy."

"No. You're wrong."

"You made a mistake, didn't you? I'm not sure what you're plotting, but I didn't go along with your invitations, so you failed at getting close to me. Not counting when we first ran into each other, I've only seen you twice. There was no time to make me love you. Am I wrong?"

"What are you saying? Let's talk about this in person. Where are you?"

"Your voice has changed. In this short a conversation, you've already asked where I am three times. I can imagine how cold your eyes must look. Bye."

I hung up. Inside, I thought this was a good choice. It felt right based on both my experience and something like intuition. But I was tired, and my emotions were wild, even though I knew there was no reason for them to be that way. I started to tear up for no reason.

"There really aren't any cars following us?" I asked the driver again. There was no point in asking. Even my voice was teary. I was uneasy, and tired.

"We're fine. If there are any cars, I'll let you know."

". . . You'd let me know, even though I might be a criminal? Even if it's the police?"

"Yes."

The car went quiet for a moment. Even after hearing my bizarre questions, the driver was strangely calm.

"After all, I'm a cab driver. I must respond to my customers' demands. Regardless of who they are, I give my customer the best service I can."

"Even if you get arrested?"

"I won't. I'd just say I had to do whatever I did. Besides, you don't seem like a bad person."

"How can you tell?"

"Hmmm."

I stared at the driver. He was old. He was a strange man. But for some reason, he made me feel a bit more comfortable.

However much we talked, once I got out of this cab, I'd never see him again. All of my relationships were like this. Even Kimura, whom I was entrusting my fate to, I didn't really know. I woke up in the cab, and realized I had dozed off for a bit. I could see the Ikebukuro Marui department store in the distance. I couldn't drag this driver into this. I got out of the cab at an intersection and put on my mask.

I COULDN'T KEEP looking behind me or I'd appear unnatural. I had put on glasses, changed my hair color and clothes, so it would be hard to tell it was me from far away. But I couldn't go to the parking lot like this. If the police were waiting there, they'd find the gun in my bag.

If I just threw it away randomly, I'd feel bad. A strange person might pick it up and use it. But there were cameras monitoring the garbage cans in front of the convenience stores. I found a mailbox and walked up to it. There were no cameras there, so I could get rid of it safely. And when a postal worker found it, they'd do the responsible thing. I put the whole bag in the box and walked away quickly.

There were a lot of police cars. I wondered if something had happened. A screen on one of the buildings was playing the news. Two diplomats had committed suicide. A certain stock's price had soared suddenly, and then dropped unnaturally. But that had nothing to do with me. If my passport wasn't there, I'd get out of Tokyo. If it was, I'd make for the airport. If they were following me, I'd just have to lose them.

The moon was rising from right behind the hotel. For some reason, I stared at it blankly. I went into the hotel, walked past the front desk, and took the elevator to the basement. My heart was beating disgustingly fast. I thought about how far I had come. But I needed to hold off on the sentimentality until after everything was over.

The elevator door opened, and I walked into the dark parking lot. There were spots where the surface of the concrete was black and wet for some reason. There were almost no cars. There was the black sedan with a Hiroshima plate. My breathing was wild, and my body freezing. No one was following me. I was fine. I just had to find out whether the passport was really there.

I held my breath. I needed to focus, to be ready for anything. I put my hand on the door. The silver handle reflected what little light there was in the dim garage. It felt cold on my fingers. The handle clicked and the door opened. It wasn't locked. I sensed someone's presence. When I turned around, a man wearing a construction worker's uniform was getting out of the elevator. I stared at him. Was he really a construction worker? He was large. I stared at him and thought about how I could get out of here if he tried something. But he never looked at me, just headed into the parking lot. Off in the distance, he picked up a brush. Something was dripping from the end of the brush. I let out a big sigh. Aside from him, there was no one around me.

I opened the driver's door, and then opened the glove

compartment. Strangely, my hand wasn't shaking. I sat in the driver's seat and felt around the compartment. My fingertips were moist. Was it there? Mixed in with all these papers was a black bag. When I looked inside, there was a passport.

I felt a dull pain in my chest. I sensed someone behind the driver's seat. Our eyes met in the rearview mirror. I couldn't move. In the back seat was Kizaki. I'm not sure why, but for some reason I felt like I had known all along that he would be there. My body went limp.

"Drive."

16.

WHEN DID I realize I would never get what I want most?

Do I still want it? If I got it, what would I do?

I WAS WALKING down an unmaintained dirt road with my backpack on. I walked as far as I could. Was I running from the orphanage? Did I just want to visit somewhere? I vaguely noticed my dirty shoes getting dirtier as I walked along that straight road, following the river.

I could see lots of lights in the distance. I had seen those lights like this, from far away, once before. Those lights belonged to the big, new shopping mall they had built in this small town. They were bright. They were so bright they made my eyes hurt.

Why was I trying to go toward those bright lights? Was it because they seemed kind? The closer I got to the lights, the more it felt like they would envelop me. I came to a brick road. It was wide enough to be a town square. There was a lit-up fountain and flowers surrounded by rows of glittering shops. From far away, I probably looked like I had made it inside that light.

It took me some time to realize that my dirty shoes stood out in all this light. I felt embarrassed. I found a bench and sat down with my backpack still on. A small boy being led by a grown man and woman passed by. He had ice cream in his hand. It was white. He looked so proud and sweet. It was beautiful. For some reason, I wanted it. But I only had seventy yen. When we kids at the orphanage said we wanted something, it made trouble for the people there. Strictly speaking, the money I had wasn't even mine.

I sat on the bench and watched everyone around me. There were couples laughing and joking. A young girl in red begging an old woman for a fish-shaped cake. Families dividing up their big paper shopping bags for everyone to carry. Children who still tried to get their parents to hold their hands, even though they were carrying those big bags. How long was I there like that? I found myself staring at a big man with wide shoulders wearing a beige sweater. His sweater looked soft, and I wanted to touch it. He waved his hand in the direction of a woman and a small girl. The girl was wearing a child's orange down jacket, and in her hand she had two beautiful balloons.

For some reason, as I watched those blue and white balloons tremble in the gentle breeze, I felt my head go blank and I got worried. The man took out a cigarette; they'd leave after he smoked it. The woman and girl walked off somewhere. That orange down jacket would have looked better on me than that girl. I'd be more beautiful than that girl, or even that woman, if I could just dress up. For some reason, that's what I thought then. The man lit his cigarette. He looked like he was enjoying it. He sat on a bench a short distance from the one I was on.

I wanted him to look at me. He wore soft-looking clothes and clean shoes. He was a big man, and his face looked kind. I stared at him. But he just looked at me briefly and then turned away.

Why did I think of this then? It wasn't quite a distant memory. It was more like a vague impression welling up inside me. There was a woman who was close to me before I went to the orphanage. I could see her smooth shoulders peeking out from her loose shirt. Her thin, seductive legs stuck out from her short skirt. Those legs looked soft. I scratched my own thighs as if I had mosquito bites. I flipped up my skirt. But that man didn't look at me. My heart started beating unbelievably fast. I pulled my skirt up little by little.

My cheeks were red, and my smile was inappropriate for a child. I was trying to remember that woman's skin. I couldn't remember her face. The man looked at me. He looked at my white, thin underwear. That was the first time my body got hot. He looked surprised. I smiled at him. I smiled at him in forgiveness of his deviant passion for a child. He got up, and I went short of breath. He looked around, then approached me. I was scared and confused, but for some reason my body grew even hotter. He touched my arm, and crouched down to make eye contact.

"You shouldn't do that," he said kindly. He smiled, disregarding my fear and confusion and the heat in my body. He didn't ignore me. Instead, he approached me with unwanted kindness. He approached me like I was a troubled child.

"Are you lost? I'll call someone." He stood quietly. I felt the beautiful silver ring on his finger graze my arm. It was cool.

It's hard to explain logically what happened inside me then. I got off the bench and suddenly took off my panties. I started bawling like I was on fire.

Maybe that was my absurd way of getting revenge. But it wasn't directed at that man. It was directed at the life that surrounded me. It was revenge on the will of the world. The will that determined everything that happened around me, regardless of how I felt. If things wouldn't go the way I wanted, I'd just have to destroy everything. Even if things did turn out the way I wanted, I should still destroy it all. Before it abandoned me, before it lost interest in me, I'd have to betray the world. I felt heat in my body. It was so hot, so hot I didn't know what to do. The man was surprised. He tried to smile even more kindly, to repel me gently. But he had no time. He had to leave me to run away, to some safe place far from me. A young man with a security guard's arm badge came running up to me, just in time to replace the first man. I described the man who *did that* to me, but he was already gone. Suddenly, I realized that the security guard was looking at me harshly. At the balled up, white underwear caught on my feet. He puffed out his cheeks a bit, and made a face I didn't like. He seemed angry. I took off my underwear and put it in my pocket.

The moon was there in the distance. Even when I was much, much younger than that, I used to stare at the moon. Why did the full moon look really red then? It shined bright and clear through the thin veil of clouds. As if praying quietly for a new beginning.

17.

I DIDN'T KNOW where I was driving.

I drove at a constant speed down a dark road. Kizaki told me three times to switch routes, and in the course of turning where he told me to, I lost track of where I was. I knew he was behind me, smiling slightly. I wondered when I had come under his control. When had I become a part of his scheme? Kizaki told me to turn, so I turned the steering wheel.

But that's not really true. I'd always been living my

own life. That should seem obvious, but sometimes I thought it was strange.

I remember when I was a kid, and this man and woman were deciding whether to become my foster parents. Listening to the staff talk to this couple, I thought their conversation seemed so precarious, like either side could collapse at any moment. It felt strange that my life could change so drastically because of other people. I turned down that couple, but was that just to reject someone else's trying to take control of my life? Or, by rejecting them, did I enter my own life?

"Hey . . ." For some reason my voice was quiet. "What are you?"

"Who knows."

We drove down a narrow alley. There were no lights. We might have been surrounded by houses or by shops.

"At that bar," he said finally, "you rejected Hasegawa's first invitation, and moved away from me. But you came back again. When you think about it, there are a lot of strange forces at work in this world."

"I . . ."

"You don't know what's happening? That's fine. I like

watching people die unsure of what's happening. I'm in a good mood, so I'll tell you some of it."

I could see streetlights in the distance. We arrived at a wide road. I was soaked in sweat.

"First of all, Yata is going to die soon. He's low on the totem pole, but he belongs to a big organization. They'll forget about him."

"What kind of organization?"

"The people who benefit from this country's gains. It's not an organization, really. More of an informal group— a class."

He lit a cigarette behind my back.

"Imagine a revolution. Imagine the people rise up and overthrow the emperor. Then new people take power. After that, people flock to those who have just seized control. The new rulers are the ones that everyone thinks have been overthrown. But only the appearance has changed. Those are the people who benefit from the gains of this country. In Japan, and outside of it, many people flock to those in power. And they maintain the system. It's a disgustingly flexible system. Even if you rip it to shreds, it will return to what it once was.

Revolution is usually just a way for the common people to let out some steam."

"And you?"

"I have my eyes on the system because I want to bring everything to a head. To rip it to bits."

"You want to end equality?"

Kizaki laughed loudly.

"Of course not. I don't care about anything as boring as that. I want to see things boil over. You should see it. It's really amazing. When those in power come under assault and cling to what they have in total confusion."

I followed Kizaki's instructions and turned down another small alley. Buildings that looked like warehouses lined the hazy darkness.

"Do you have any other questions? Is that all?"

"What about Hasegawa?"

"He's not the Hasegawa you knew. He's his older brother."

"What?"

"They had different mothers. When you came to that orphanage, he had already been sent to a foster home.

When I learned about you, the woman who was paying all this money for a kid named Shota, the woman who does this strange work, I happened to see his name as well, from the same orphanage."

My vision narrowed.

"I thought I'd have him approach you just in case you tried to run. Wouldn't it have been great if you ran to him for help and I was there?"

He chuckled. Something like loneliness suddenly surged through me.

"I guess he didn't have the right attitude for it."

"He can take on any personality. He seems to have been born a compulsive liar. I've heard he seems especially kind when he's helping others out. He doesn't consider the destruction that comes afterward. He seems to get drunk on his own kindness when he's helping someone, but then, afterward, he gets angry. He wonders why they aren't unhappy. And then he tears them apart. He does exactly as much bad as he does good. But he looks so sweet."

These twisted people. This whole place was unbelievably twisted. But that had probably drawn out my twistedness as well.

"How great. There were several possible cases. All these forking paths, but they all ran in the same general direction. It's impressive, and I'm really surprised that you made it this far, but this is the end of the end. You kept betraying people, and in the end you can't escape. Get out here."

The ground was covered in cement and there was nothing but warehouses. It seemed like it was all sinking into the darkness. A little ways away was a port. I could smell the sea. We were at a harbor. Far, far away I could see the faint glow of a lighthouse. The light that guides boats through the distance. That powerful light might have been a trap.

I leaned my back against the car and looked at Kizaki. I couldn't do anything more than stand there. Kizaki pressed the gun in his right hand straight against the exact center of my forehead.

"Do you believe in fate?"

Everything around us was silent. There was no one besides us. I could only hear his voice.

"I control your fate. Or you could say your fate is to be controlled by me. But that's the same thing either way, isn't it?"

Kizaki pressed his hand to my chest.

"This, this heart that brought you here. This heart that was in the very center of the center of your life. It's beating the most wildly it has ever beaten. It's saying 'I want to live!' It's saying 'Stop!'"

It was as if everything inside me was flowing out through the hand on my chest and entering into him.

"Will I shoot, or won't I? If there really is such a thing as fate, and if it knows what will become of all humans' lives, my consciousness is joining that giant, divine fate. Ha ha ha. My consciousness is becoming one with the power that does whatever it wants with your life. This powerful, unforgiving providence. Will I shoot? Won't I? This moment must be unbearable."

Kizaki suddenly brought his face to mine.

"Or will you become my toy? Will you try to seduce me? With everything you have."

The moon was full behind him. It was shining red. For some reason, it was so red I didn't know what to do. My lips, which had touched his before, grew hot as if they were struggling to live. That heat forced its way through my entire body. Even given these circumstances, the heat in me grew so strong that my life didn't matter. It was as if it had a will of its own. *Inside you.* Suddenly, I remembered those words. They didn't seem to be coming from the moon in front of me, or from within me. My body was hot. It was so hard to breathe, my eyes grew cloudy. Now I was trying consciously to remember those words. The moon was shining bright. It was shining so bright I didn't know what to do. *This boy, inside you.*

Staring blankly at the moon, feeling the heat inside me, I recollected my life up until that moment. It was exactly as if I had led my trivial life just so I could come here. As if everything inside me, all the wounds, they were all little necessities. It was like we were on that boat I could see in the distance, and he was touching my body gently. Those bloody fingers he raised cruelly against all humanity touched only me gently. His tongue entered my open mouth. He made me take off my clothes piece by piece. He wrapped his big, sweaty arms around me. I felt his heavy body with my whole being. As those necessary, overfull sensations surrounded me, he entered me. He pierced me. Violently. Powerfully. Like he was going to break me. I wailed. My arms wrapped around him. I opened my legs to make it easier for him, to let him in deeper. He was filled with joy because of my body. I came over and over again, as if I was on fire. It was like a festival to pray for the birth of new life. I cried. He pierced me. I clung to him, crying. He was all the way inside me. He stayed there so long, so long. He let out a sudden breath. I grabbed his shoulders and took all of his sperm inside me. I took it, over and over again.

Once he has seized control of the very core of this earth, I will kill him. I will make my child the king of this dark world. That sudden, enormous betrayal will make my body so hot it will shine like fire. A heat you can never experience in everyday life. In that moment, I will be the most beautiful thing shining on this earth. Next to his corpse, I will shine more beautifully, more freely than anyone or anything. That is the moment I will get it. I will make that powerful, black light that looks down on this whole earth mine. I will claim that heat. That moment that envelops everything. I will claim that powerful darkness. That beautiful, shining darkness that stands over the world, cruel and proud.

FUMINORI NAKAMURA

"But."

Suddenly, I began to cry. It wouldn't be like that, I realized. I felt that things wouldn't turn out that way. I kept crying. I told the man in front of me pointing a gun to my head, "But if I became your woman, wouldn't I die a cruel death? Probably one even more awful than if you kill me now. Not everything can go according to plan. Maybe you'll spare only your child and kill me for no reason. You could show me everything I left unfinished . . . And then you'd kill me as I burn with desire. It would be like I lived my life just to have your child, and once that job is done . . ."

He kept staring at me. "That might be true."

I shook my head. I kept shaking my head. Like a child about to explode with discontent, like a baby trying to get its way. He slowly pulled down the hammer of the gun with his thumb. The whole arm holding the gun tensed.

"There's one final thing you should know. *The thing you think you want most is not necessarily what you truly want.* Humans are like that."

Kizaki's shoulders grew tense. He moved suddenly. I

tried to say something, but I couldn't speak. It couldn't be true. I knew what was happening, but none of it felt real. I tried to find the strength to scream. Was this the sound of an explosion? I couldn't see the moon anymore. My ears were hot. But, for some reason, I could still see Kizaki in front of me.

"*Think calmly*. Do you really think I'd go out of my way to kill someone like you?"

Kizaki was smiling. I stared blankly at his thin eyes behind his sunglasses. Was the liquid flowing down my ear blood? I couldn't understand what was happening.

"*I'll let you live. In exchange for your life.*"

Kizaki lowered the gun. My whole body relaxed, and I sat down right there. My shoulders were shaking. I couldn't control my body.

"You will take responsibility for several small crimes involved in this incident . . . As someone already dead. To obscure our participation in the incident, and to *make things make sense*."

My mind was still blank, but I tried to stand up.

"*I will rewrite your life*. Your whole past. Yours will be the story of the death of a beautiful prostitute who worked behind the scenes of several incidents. We will make you take responsibility for several of our crimes. *You will lose the whole life you led*, but you we will spare your life."

I could see the moon in the distance.

"Rather than leaving behind a *corpse*, you'll use that passport to become a different person and disappear. That turned out to be better for us. There's something amazing about the way you clung to your life. You're interesting. So we'll let you live."

For some reason the moon grew calm. It was as if the light shining until a moment ago was only temporary. I could hear a boat's engine in the distance. The sea was trembling. I noticed that the wind felt cold on my cheeks and neck. My body was still shaking. I couldn't stand up.

"This was all meaningless. I get to go free for no reason at all. I . . ."

"There is a reason. It's a stupid one, though. Revenge. Revenge for that child's death."

Kizaki looked at me coldly.

"You couldn't save his life, so, like an idiot, you came

to hate anything you couldn't explain. And you resisted the things around you that you couldn't understand. This time it was your own life on the line, but that didn't really matter. You'd've taken it as a loss if anyone's life was stolen without reason."

"I couldn't save that child."

"How stupid," Kizaki said, exasperated. "It's not a question of good and bad. You made such a fuss, that useless child managed to get better temporarily. He was so pathetic, but he managed to stand on his own two legs again. Someone probably told him that the world needed people like him. He may have even thought he'd actually get better. You see, it's not a question of what's good and what's bad. *What's important* is savoring all that he experienced."

"You said something similar when you were talking about your theory of evil."

"They're the front and back of the same coin. That's why you should have smiled and enjoyed your sadness at his death. The death of a child is a wonderful thing."

"I can't do that."

I could see several cars in the shadow of one of the

warehouses some ways off. Their lights were pointed down, and they were coming toward us.

"I had planned on seeing you off, but guess I can't. Do what you like with that car," Kizaki said. He began to walk away.

"Wait. Really?"

The cars grew gradually closer.

"Don't make me say it again. I don't care what you do with your life. How egotistical."

He didn't bother to look at me.

"Thank me privately. Well, I guess you won't thank me. I took your life away." He kept talking, though he seemed bored. *"Who am I who took your life away?* Think about it. Hide yourself somewhere. Leave the country once everything calms down. You can't become a different person with just a passport. I'll have my men prepare the other documents. I'll pardon you for the pleasure I got from your making it all the way to the end. Consider it thanks for helping with the destruction of Yata. Go. If you're not satisfied, just show yourself to me again. You're a great way to waste time. Next time, I might kill you."

"What will you do?"

"I'm not doing anything. I'm going back to the show."

He turned from me lazily. I wondered if he'd ever look at me again.

"But will you ever be fulfilled? Don't you just feel empty?"

"You still don't understand anything." Kizaki laughed suddenly. "Then you just have to enjoy the emptiness. That's the only answer in this world."

He walked toward the black cars. He abandoned me there without looking back.

I realized I had a faint memory of this scene. The back of someone who abandoned me when I was small. I was too young to say what I wanted. I was still very little, but I remember watching that person walk away. Little by little, that memory bubbled up inside me. That calm scene was probably the beginning of my life.

It was as if my life was bookended by this scene. Like some sort of strange cycle.

18.

THE AIRPORT AT night. It was crowded.

I couldn't take my knife on the plane, so I hid it in my checked bag. I wondered if they'd take it. I wouldn't use it for anything, but I felt uncomfortable without it. I didn't have confidence in my ability to live on without it.

The news was on repeat on the TV in the waiting area for the boarding gate. Several more diplomats had killed themselves, and a bunch of Diet members and local officials had either killed themselves or stepped down from their positions. Ambassadors from other countries staying in Japan were also being swapped out, and the stock market and the value of the yen continue to rise and fall unnaturally. Several people from the financial world had gone missing. The announcer continued his broadcast, speaking passionately. While I watched the news, I wondered absentmindedly whether Yata was still alive. Kizaki said Yata would die, but for some reason, I thought he was still alive. Yata wasn't the type to die so easily. Maybe he'd hidden himself somewhere and was waiting, silently, for something. I didn't know what he'd be waiting for, but for some reason, I imagined he was.

I felt thirsty, so I bought black tea from a vending machine. Behind the large plane waiting to take off, the moon was shining, almost full.

What was the moon then? Was it just my fantasy? An illusion that suddenly came to my scared, tired body? Or maybe that illusion tried to fool me, but I didn't let it. I kept staring at the moon. I'm not sure if its light was good or evil. I thought it might not be either. The moon just shines with the light of chaos. Mysteriously.

Brightly. That must not be either good or evil. Just as the rules of this world are not all good.

The earth will block the sun little by little, and the moon will gradually shrink until it finally disappears. Just as if it can't bear all of its own energy. Ancient people grew worried when the moon vanished, and held festivals to pray for its return. The moon appeared again. Just a thin crescent, but clearly shining. But, still, that did not reassure the ancient people. They were scared that instead of growing fuller, that thin light would vanish again. So they held more festivals to reassure themselves.

A man might appear out of nowhere at any moment and shoot me. Even now, someone might be watching me from a distance. I couldn't say that I was safe yet. He knew my new name. When I arrived overseas I'd have to find another name.

Was this the same moon I saw then? My life was taken by that man, but now I'm sitting here like this. Something enormous passed right by me, and I still haven't completely regained control of my body. I remembered that man walking away. What was that exhausting sadness I felt then? It was like I witnessed a story I had lost. That story fit between the essential scenes that bookend my life. But then I started again from that scene. I'm not a child anymore. I have no choice but to live. All I have left is my life. I thought about rebirth, and laughed. To be abandoned is the same thing as to be free. I set myself free with my own hands. Can't I do anything for all the people struggling in this suffocating world? I'm not sure what I could do, but anything would be fine. Something that suited me. Like helping children like Shota cheat their fate.

And if one day I could return to Tokyo, I would walk through that city. I remembered that man with the long fingers who stole my knife. I could probably tell him what happened if I could find him again. What would he say? I wonder if he'd tell me what happened to him.

What tide was I being tossed around by? Who or what had I betrayed? What had I escaped from?

From now on, I had to start putting in my time again. The next time some great force like that comes to me, will I take hold of it?

—

OUT OF NOWHERE, a man in a suit came walking toward me. For some reason, that big man drew my attention. I lost my breath. My pulse went wild. He didn't look like he would turn at the corner. He was walking straight toward me. I had no time to think about what to do. I grabbed my bag and started to stand up, but then I saw a woman waving at him. He joined her and they walked into a busy shop. I exhaled. The old person sitting in front of me turned, surprised by my sudden movement. There was no helping it. I'd be like this for a while.

The kid sitting caddy corner from me was crying. He was asking his mother for something, and she refused. The mother was ugly, but the child had a beautiful face. My eyes met the child's. His crying face was funny to me for some reason, and I smiled slightly. At first, I thought he looked like Shota. Then I realized he didn't look like Shota at all. The mother went to the bathroom. The child was still crying.

I got up from my seat. I moved my clumsy body carefully, faced the child, and crouched down so our eyes would meet. The child was surprised, and looked at me strangely. Of course he did. A tired, gaudy-looking woman had just appeared out of nowhere. He didn't look like he'd stop crying for anything.

He looked at the vending machine at the edge of his vision, and stared at the tea in my hands. "You want this?" When I asked, he made a serious face, looked at the tea, and began to reach his small hands out. But then he hesitated. I smiled. Heat spread through my body.

"Don't worry. It's not poison."

AUTHOR'S AFTERWORD

THIS IS MY tenth novel.

When I was working on *The Thief*, I thought I wanted to write not a sequel but a sister novel. Two novels where you could read either one first, or even just enjoy one on its own.

If you enjoyed this novel, I'd be happy if you picked up *The Thief* as well. There are a lot of connections between the two, and I think you'll enjoy them. That, however, is just my hope as a novelist. There are the same number of chapters in *The Kingdom* as *The Thief*, and the page counts differ only by one page. That was a complete accident, of course. It seems that these two novels just needed to be written that way. When writing novels, these kinds of coincidences sometimes occur.

I began by saying simply this is my tenth novel, but

ten is a very serious number. I'm glad that I could write this novel at this major juncture.

Thank you everyone who helped me with this book. Thank you everyone who reads it. I have only made it this far because of my readers' support. Thank you very much.

Nakamura Fuminori, September 2, 2011

BIBLIOGRAPHY

Cashford, Jules. *The Moon: Myth and Image [Tsuki no bunka shi]*. Translation by Sadanori Bekku and Sachiko Katayanagi. Shufusha.

Kanji, Hayashi. *The Book of the Moon [Tsuki no hon]*. Kadokawa.

Motokawa, Shirao. *Basics of the Moon [Tsuki no kihon]*. Seibundo-Shinkosha.

Unno, Hiroshi. *Supai no sekai shi [The History of the World of Spies]*. Bungei Shunju.

Violane, Vanoyeke. *La Prostitution en Grece et a Rome [Shofu no rekishi]*. Translation by Hisako Hashiguchi. Harashobo.

These works among others were used as reference for this book.